the

MARQUESS
takes a
BRIDE

JR SALISBURY

OLIVER
HEBER
BOOKS

All rights reserved.

No part of this publication may be sold, copied, distributed, reproduced or transmitted in any form or by any means, mechanical or digital, including photocopying and recording or by any information storage and retrieval system without the prior written permission of both the publisher, Oliver Heber Books and the author, JR Salisbury, except in the case of brief quotations embodied in critical articles and reviews.

PUBLISHER'S NOTE: This is a work of fiction. Names, characters, places, and incidents either are the product of the author's imagination or are used fictitiously. Any resemblance to actual persons, living or dead, business establishments, events, or locales is entirely coincidental.

© Jamie Salisbury

Cover Design by Wicked Smart Designs

Published by Oliver-Heber Books

0 9 8 7 6 5 4 3 2 1

CHAPTER 1

"***D***id you accept the Duke and Duchess of Hampshire's invitation?" Viscount Radstock asked as he accepted another whiskey from a tall, lanky footman. The pair had gotten together at White's, along with the Earl of Preston, one evening to pass the time.

Percival Montgomery, the Marquess of Trent took a long sip of whiskey while considering his answer. His black hair was combed back and in a queue, longer than the fashionable short style a lot of men preferred.

"I have. I might not have accepted, but the duke is a close friend of my father's, so I felt obligated since my parents are going on holiday," Trent replied. He finished his whiskey and motioned to the footman to bring him another.

"And so it begins," Preston said lazily. "The endless balls, soirees, teas, and God knows whatever else we're expected to attend."

"Amen," Radstock concurred. He polished off his whiskey and waited while a footman brought him yet another.

"Fortunately for me, I'm needed at Trent Manor. I'm in the middle of some minor renovations."

"How long will you be?" Preston inquired, swirling the contents in his glass.

"I've planned for a week, no more. I hope the renovations will be completed by the time I leave to head back to London."

"I understand Lady Hamilton's father has granted her another season," Radstock said.

"I've heard as much from my sister," Trent said before finishing his whiskey. He set the glass down on a table next to him. "I imagine the duke is anxious to see her married."

Preston leaned forward in his chair. The three of them were the last of a larger group of friends from Cambridge who still remained unmarried. "Perhaps you won't have to look far for your betrothed."

Trent shook his head. "No. Lady Eugenie is the last lady I would take as a wife."

"Why is that?" Radstock inquired with a lopsided grin.

"That's a long story. One for another time."

"Lady Eugenie and Trent grew up together. Her father, the Duke of Brandon's estate runs alongside that of Trent's family," Preston said with a snicker.

Trent shook his head. He hated being teased like this, always had. It would be one thing if his friends were good-natured about it, but once they got hold of something like Lady Eugenie, they wouldn't let it go. They were like a couple of dogs with a prized bone.

"Yes, we saw each other during the summer. Couldn't help not to, the way she raced her horse across both estates."

"Well, you won't be able to avoid her. Not during the season. Not unless you want to go hide out at Trent Manor for the entire season. You're bound to run into her," Radstock said.

Preston snorted as he finished his whiskey. "She

must be unpleasant to look at if Trent wishes to avoid her."

Trent again shook his head and took yet another glass of whiskey from a footman. He hadn't intended to drink, at least not more than a glass or two, but these two were relentless. "I can assure you that the last time I laid eyes on Lady Eugenie she was quite pleasant to look at."

"Interesting," Preston said.

"Come, let's talk of other things. Like the two of you finding brides this season," Trent said with a snicker. He peered at his friends over the top of his glass. Good, they were uncomfortable with the subject. Why he wasn't sure, but they both avoided any discussion about marriage like the plague. "There will be a brand new crop of debutantes to choose from if one of the other more seasoned young ladies doesn't suit you."

"Well, you know good and well why I haven't," Radstock said irritably. "I'm destined to marry Lady Lucinda."

"But when? You two have yet to set a date," Preston said.

"Lady Lucinda promised me when she and her family return from the continent, we would set a date."

"And when will they be returning, and better yet, why did they go with the season starting?" Trent asked.

Radstock had been born to marry Lady Lucinda Buckingham. It was an arranged marriage, one decided upon when both were still in leading strings. The big hurdle for both was that neither particularly liked the other. Trent was thankful his parents had never resorted to something as cold as an arranged marriage. Probably because his parents' marriage was not arranged. They had fallen in love, almost at first sight, and to this day were inseparable.

"Lady Lucinda's aunt, her mother's sister, was

gravely ill. The last letter I received from her said her aunt was much improved and that she and her parents were heading back to London next week."

"Let the wedding plans begin," Preston crowed.

"Yes, it's past time we married. Perhaps Preston and I will have luck finding our brides this season," Trent added.

"Speak for yourself," Preston replied. "I'm not quite ready to become chained to any one woman."

"What about your mistress?" Trent asked with a smile.

"That's different."

Trent laughed and finished his whiskey. He rose from his chair and looked at his friend. "Keep telling yourself that. Anyway, the hour grows late."

"Will we see you before you leave for Trent Manor?" Preston inquired lazily, a sure sign he was relaxed.

"I'm not leaving until the day after the Hampshire affair."

"Excellent. I'm planning on going to Tattersall's tomorrow if either of you are interested," Radstock offered.

"Let me check my schedule in the morning," Trent replied. He tipped his head. "Gentlemen, stay out of trouble." Trent walked through the smoke-filled room and to the outside where he waited for a boy to bring him his stallion. Tattersall's would indeed be a good diversion, even if he only looked. He enjoyed good horseflesh, and there was plenty that went through their doors.

He swung his leg over Solomon's back and headed toward Trent House, his home here in London. He'd purchased the house a year ago, even though he could have continued staying at the family home. The house had been a solid investment and a place where he could be himself, away from the probing eyes of his parents and grandmother when she traveled to London. Which she did when the season first started. She lived for the gossip and goings-on of the ton.

He began to navigate the stallion through the heavy London traffic. It was slow on any given night, but now with the Season about to begin, carriages dominated the streets. Which was why he preferred to ride his stallion when the weather cooperated.

It didn't take him long until he reached his new home in Mayfair. He enjoyed its close location to Hyde Park, where he could ride his stallion or take his curricle out for a drive. It was also near Bond Street and Seville Row, where his tailor and other shops he frequented were located.

An admirer of fine architecture, Trent had jumped at the opportunity to purchase this elegant Georgian townhouse. It rose four stories in front and, similar to his estate in Gloucestershire, was made of ashlar blocks.

He dismounted quickly and handed the reins over to a sleepy looking stable boy who'd been waiting for him to return so he might take Solomon back to the mews and his stall.

Trent handed his great coat, gloves, and hat over to Mills, his butler, who'd come with the property when he'd purchased the townhouse. He was tall and slim with the hawk nose that so many butlers seemed to have. Better for looking down at people.

"I placed a letter on your desk, my lord."

"Who would be sending me correspondence this late at night?" Trent mused as he began to walk up the stairs and in the direction of his study.

"The letter came from your father's house; that's what I got from the boy who brought it," Mills replied.

"Is the boy waiting for a reply?"

"No, my lord. I sent him on his way. I told him since

the hour was late if a reply were needed immediately, I would send someone from the house."

"Excellent. I shall find you should I need to respond this evening," Trent replied. He continued to walk in the direction of his study.

He entered his study and found a fire burning in the hearth. He spied a silver tray sitting in the middle of the mahogany desk. Before he acted on whatever was in the missive, Trent walked over to a table and picked up a crystal decanter of whiskey and poured himself a glass. He took a sip before he strode across the room to his desk.

Picking up the missive, he broke the seal and began to read. He started to laugh. It was an invitation, or rather he was being commanded, to dinner the following evening at the family's London home. His father made mention to Trent that if he valued not only his own, but his father's life, he would make sure to be there promptly. His mother was one short and thought he would be an excellent choice.

He took another swallow of whiskey before finding paper and a pen. He wrote out his reply. Yes, he would attend as he had nothing planned for the evening. He wondered as he folded the letter who exactly would be attending. Not that it mattered. He knew most all of his parents' friends, even those in London. It might be good to see some of the men. His father had a good friend in the Duke of Leicester, who had only recently remodeled his country estate. Perhaps the duke might have some insight into what and how he should do things at his own home.

Luckily for him, this townhouse had been freshly painted and updated before he'd purchased it. It was going to be hard enough to endure one major remodel. He wasn't sure he could deal with two going on at the same time.

He sat back in his chair and closed his eyes. There was no sound except the fire sparking in the hearth. It was probably the most peaceful thing he'd heard in quite a while. His parents' home was always a beehive of activity. Even with his sister Caroline married and living in Scotland, there was always something going on. His mother fully believed one couldn't be idle when in London.

Here he could enjoy a peaceful evening such as this with no one to speak to or listen to. He liked the idea of having control of his life. Not that he didn't; it was just when the family was in London, his mother always had something planned and expected him to make an appearance at most of her events.

As much as he hated to admit it, it was time he perhaps took a more serious interest in finding a wife. He wasn't getting any younger, and he needed to be wed and start a nursery of his own. Still, he would miss the freedom of being single. Then there was his idea on the matter of love. He wasn't sure if love actually existed or if it was merely the bond between two people who felt comfortable around each other. Nor did he want a loveless marriage where the only time he visited his wife's bed was to try and make a child. Wives like these were more than likely to be cold in their affections towards their husbands. He certainly didn't want this and would rather see himself single than in a cold marriage.

Most of his friends, with the exception of Preston and Radstock, had married. Some were arranged marriages, and the couples had learned to respect each other. True love was seldom seen in this sort of marriage. Others were blissfully happy, and others were developing deeper feelings for their spouse as time went on. He would love to find himself happy with one woman; it would make life so much more tolerable. But where would he find such a woman?

With the season starting up, he decided the best measure would be to sit back and observe the young ladies first. He wasn't keen on a young debutante, either, one in her first season. As he was approaching his thirtieth year, he would have little in common with a doe-eyed debutante.

CHAPTER 2

$\mathcal{L}$ ady Eugenie Hamilton detested having to stay in London any longer than was absolutely necessary. In London, one must be on their best behavior because there was always someone, somewhere watching you, waiting for you to fall out of step. All so they could gossip, and the ton loved to do just that.

Besides that, she couldn't ride as freely as she could at home at Brandon Manor. Here it was expected she have a chaperone, or at least a groom, ride with her. In the country, she could outrun and frustrate all her father's grooms. Preferring to ride astride at home, she certainly couldn't do that in Hyde Park without raising some eyebrows. No, sidesaddle was considered the preferred saddle of the genteel sex.

Added to her list of dislikes of London had to be the endless parties, musicales, balls, and teas. Not that she minded them in small doses, but not almost every night, depending on what invitations her parents had accepted. She liked her solitude so she could sit and read in the library or play piano for herself, and no one else, in the music room.

Now tonight, it began. They were invited to dinner

at the home of the Duke and Duchess of Marlborough. The duke and duchess were old friends of her parents, and their country estate ran alongside Brandon Manor. She'd known both Lady Caroline and Lord Percival, now the Marquess of Trent, growing up. She wondered if they would be in attendance. It would be good to see them. At least it would be nice to visit with Lady Caroline; however, she had recently married, and Eugenie was unsure whether or not she and her husband would be in attendance.

She smiled, thinking of Trent. He never had been able to keep up with her when they rode during the summers. Not even the last time when he rode that magnificent stallion of his, but then Trent had always had an eye for exceptional horseflesh, so it didn't surprise her when he showed up a couple of summers ago riding the black beast.

She reminded herself to be polite when he did speak to her. Too much conversation might have both sets of parents hoping there might be a chance at a match between them. Not that she'd ever encouraged such foolishness before.

What Trent needed was some doe-eyed debutante or one perhaps a year or two older. A woman pleasant to look at—one who could carry out the most minimal of conversations and most importantly, one who would bear him an heir and fill his nursery. What she didn't wish was for him to have a wife who actually enjoyed the marital bed. Mustn't wish him too much satisfaction in that aspect of marriage. Besides, he would turn into just another aristocratic gentleman who kept a mistress or two on the side.

This would be her second season, having been able to sit out the year before, partially in luck due to the death of her grandmother, the dowager Duchess of Brandon. Unfortunately, her parents had granted her another season, but it came with certain stipulations and expectations. She needed to find a potential suitor to court her, and a marriage was, of course, an unspoken must.

Little did she know, her parents already had someone in mind.

Her thoughts were quickly crushed by the sound of her lady's maid entering the room.

"Are you ready to dress, my lady?" Mona Babcock asked. The woman had been her grandmother's lady's maid, and her father immediately thought the older woman was more of what his daughter needed. Relationships between servants and the aristocratic family they served was looked down upon.

Eugenie's last maid had been a young girl, Trish White, who suddenly ran off with one of her father's grooms. Eugenie had encouraged the young girl to follow her heart, and the maid took her words to heart.

"I suppose I'd best," she replied. "You have the periwinkle gown ready?"

"Of course, my lady. I also have had a bath drawn."

Eugenie smiled. "Thank you. Will I have time for a good soak? I wouldn't want to smell of horses, would I? Papa would surely frown upon that."

"Yes, you have plenty of time if you go now," Babcock replied.

Eugenie started toward the bathing chamber. "You laid out the orange blossom scented soap Mama got me while she was in Paris?"

"But of course, my lady."

"Excellent."

A few moments later she climbed into the large porcelain tub and sighed. The water was heavenly. She submerged herself beneath the surface to wet her hair. It wouldn't take long to dry if she sat in front of the fire as soon as she finished. Babcock had made sure she had plenty of time for extras like this.

Then she would be stuffed into a corset and petticoats and finally into her gown. Her hair would be swept up in a fashionable style, and she would be ready to present herself to her family and their guests, right on time.

As all women of her age did, they dressed and readied to present themselves to any potential suitors and their families. The problem with tonight is she knew everyone quite well. Still her mother, the Duchess of Brandon, expected only the best out of her.

Her brother Edward was the lucky one; he was abroad on his grand tour as her father called it. Eugenie knew it for what it really was. A time to frolic and savor things with just the two friends who accompanied him. Who was it he took? Ah yes, Thomas Levy, Viscount Titus, and Andrew Upton, Marquess of Fuller. Both longtime friends and partners in debauchery for as long as she could remember. Never, ever would she consider either of these two as a potential husband.

The viscount's father had spent most of Thomas's fortune, gambled away in gaming clubs. The rumors weren't pretty, his father's creditors taking most everything that wasn't entailed. The only way he'd finished university and this male bonding experience was through the generosity of his uncle.

The Marquess, Andrew was known to enjoy his brandy a tiny bit too much. He already had a reputation of constantly being in his cups, but surprisingly, no one seemed to think a thing about it, thinking he would outgrow it. Eugenie knew better. Men didn't change; they didn't outgrow anything. The loftier the title, the more blind they were to the real world.

Eugenie intended to enjoy the season as much as

she possibly could. She would manage through all the boring teas, dress fittings, and other things her mother no doubt had planned for her. She'd seek out old friends, girls she could sit with on the sidelines of the ballrooms. Unfortunately, she hadn't had the time, nor the courage to write them. She wondered what Lady Felicity and Lady Abigail were doing. They loved when the season began, full of hopes and expectations of finding the perfect husband.

All Eugenie wanted in return for all the endless hours of being dressed and paraded was to be allowed to ride or even visit places that held her interest, such as the Museum of Natural History. Though it was never discouraged, it was also never encouraged as a place a young lady of her rank should wish to visit. Luckily, her father saw it as a tradeoff for all the endless hours his daughter had to endure in the company of so many women of the ton. He understood she needed time for herself, but he also knew his daughter would do what she was told and marry whoever was chosen for her if she failed to make a match on her own.

She paused in front of the mirror and took one last look before turning and heading downstairs to face her parents' guests. She was going to need all the strength she could muster to get through all this.

TRENT TURNED around the moment Lady Eugenie had been announced by the butler. He'd been engaged in a conversation with his father and the Duke of Brandon. Something about the railways and their usefulness.

This was not the Eugenie he remembered. The Lady Eugenie he remembered was nothing like the one who filled the room. This lady was blossoming into a most beautiful woman. She was still confident and held herself with grace and poise. Her reddish blond hair was swept off her shoulders, showing off a long erotic looking neck. He immediately admonished himself for thinking such thoughts but continued to watch her every move. Her deep blue eyes sparkled as she approached his mother. She was gracious and attentive to the duchess.

Then she turned and faced him as he stood with their two fathers. He wondered when the last time he'd laid eyes on her had been. More than a year. It had been in the country, and she'd tried to best him in a race across the meadows of the Marlborough estate. He knew her gelding was no match for Solomon, so he'd let her win.

She made the proposal the older gentlemen were presenting to him all the more acceptable. She would make an incredible wife and marchioness, and when the transition came, she would be a remarkable duchess. Never had he seen a young woman so secure in herself, which told him she'd be perfect.

Now all that had been left to do, if he accepted the wild proposition, was get her to trust him and agree to the marriage.

The older gentlemen had agreed to wait and let Eugenie have some of the fun that came with the Season before presenting how her life was going to change. Her father doubted Eugenie would find a husband on her own. There was always something wrong with every man she'd come in contact with.

But how would she react when told a husband had been found for her?

Though their conversation hadn't finished with Lady Eugenie's arrival, it was understood she would be given a fortnight to see who, if anyone, she seemed to fancy before being told. Trent reminded himself during this time he needed to be as gracious as possible whenever he met her. Dance with her at the balls, talk with her, and get to know her better. He'd rather he do it on his own than for a pending marriage with him being presented another way. At least if he could win her over on her own, everything would go much easier.

Let her believe things were happening on her own terms.

"Lady Eugenie, you look radiant as ever," he murmured over her gloved hand.

"Lord Trent, I wasn't sure if you would make it or not. You must be terribly busy with your new estate and all."

"Never too busy, but yes. Trent Manor is keeping me occupied when I'm in the country," he replied.

He noted nothing of the old Eugenie he once rode and laughed with. This version was more mature and grown up.

"Do you still ride as fierce as you did?" he asked.

The corner of her mouth curled up in a demure smile. "Some things will never change, my lord."

Her father interrupted, "Perhaps Lord Trent might take you riding in Hyde Park some morning. He's the only one who can keep up with you."

Before either he or Lady Eugenie could reply to her father's comment, the butler announced dinner. He offered his arm, as the two older dukes went in search of their wives across the room.

"Knowing my mother, she has us seated together. She mentioned something about not seating by rank this one time."

He nodded politely. "As we're the youngest guests, I would assume she would. I can't imagine you spending an entire supper talking with my father."

"Your father's a delightful man," she replied.

"He is for the most part. Remember, he's a duke just like your own. They get what they want."

"Are you looking forward to becoming duke, my lord?"

"It's what I've been raised to do, though the manner in which I'll become duke isn't something I look forward to."

"How's that?"

Trent bent down enough to whisper his reply. No need anyone else hear his thoughts of the matter. "My father must die before I can assume the dukedom."

"Well, don't think of that. Focus on all the good times the two of you've had," she replied. "You have had memorable times with him, haven't you?"

"Yes."

He led her to her place, and sure enough, he had been seated next to Lady Eugenie. Obviously, this was indeed a ploy for the two of them to reacquaint.

There was a lot at stake with the two families joining. The two dukes wanted to give the railway right of way on the southern side of their estates, but could only do it if they both agreed, and then it would be two sets of negotiations. An arranged marriage would benefit the two families this way, and the railway access was only the beginning. It would be a lot easier if Lady Eugenie thought a marriage with him would help out her father. There were other reasons an arranged marriage now would be beneficial, but she didn't need to know.

They had just finished the soup and were awaiting the fish to be set in front of them. Lady Eugenie had engaged in small talk with his mother who sat across the table, when she turned to him. "I understand you purchased an estate in Gloucestershire? Am I correct?"

"Yes, it is next door to Trent Manor, to the west. The house was built in the late eighteenth century."

"You speak fondly of it."

"Yes," he replied as he sat back to allow the footman to place his plate in front of him. "I am fascinated with architecture anyway, and this is a marvel to look at or even go through."

She picked up her fork. "Perhaps sometime I might see this new house. I'm sure there may well be a reason for my father to visit you. Perhaps to look at one of the fine horses I understand you breed."

"I'm sure that could be arranged, my lady," he replied before taking a bite of the salmon.

"I would like that."

He noted she was pushing her fish around on the plate before deciding where to get a piece from. Evidently, Lady Eugenie wasn't a fan of cream sauce on her fish.

"Is the fish not to your liking?" he whispered.

"It is fine."

"Liar."

"Alright. I'm not particularly fond of fish. Happy now?"

He leaned closer. "I can have one of the footmen remove the plate if it offends you."

She arched a brow. "I'm fine. It doesn't offend me. I'm just not fond of fish as I believe I just mentioned."

"Very well," he replied.

They spent the rest of the meal in relative silence, and what they did talk about was vague and safe. It was only when a dessert which included fruit and cheese was served did he feel safe to speak of matters other than the weather and roses. Roses, he remembered, were a passion of Lady Eugenie's.

"Are you attending the Duke and Duchess of Hampshire's ball Thursday evening?"

"Yes. Why do you ask?"

He looked down, anywhere but at her, as she delicately took a strawberry and took a slow, agonizing bite. She was teasing him, playing coy.

"No reason. It's supposed to be quite a feat to be invited I understand. My parents are leaving to go to the continent, so I thought I'd be a good son and represent the family."

"Really? Interesting because I heard your mother tell mine that they had postponed their holiday until early autumn."

"I beg pardon? They hadn't informed me of their change in plans." He hated that she caught him off guard. Something as huge as postponing their holiday was something he should have been informed about.

He noted the corners of her mouth turned up. She was enjoying this. It pleased her that she had information that even he didn't have, and it rubbed him the wrong way.

"You really didn't know, did you?"

"I'm quite busy. I'm sure my father would have said something tonight."

She put the remainder of the berry back on her plate. "Is it my imagination, or is something at play here."

"I don't know what you mean. Explain yourself."

"I feel as though there are things going on around me, things I've yet to be informed of."

Trent sucked in a breath. "I've had that exact feeling at various times in my life. I'm sure it's nothing."

She leaned toward him. "You are aware that my parents wish to see me at least betrothed by the end of this season."

"Mine wish me married as well. Doesn't mean it's going to happen on their schedule," he replied. "I'll marry when, and if, I choose."

"How noble," she bit off sarcastically. "And I intend

to marry for love, not for something my parents think is beneficial for me."

Her father chose just that time to rise, meaning dinner was finished. The ladies would retire to the drawing room for tea while the men remained to enjoy their port and cigars. A disgusting ritual, but it was the way things were.

She granted Trent a smile before retreating from the table with the two women.

Trent accepted a glass from his host as the door closed behind the ladies. He swirled its contents around as he waited for the interrogation to begin. This wasn't going to be accomplished easily. Lady Eugenie had already set the parameters, and she wasn't going to be coerced into anything. Not right away.

"Did you make any progress with my daughter?"

The two dukes were almost glaring at him. In their eyes, from where they stood, the task should be easy. But they were dukes, and dukes commanded the world around them. They were used to snapping their fingers and getting what they wanted. They expected no less from him. He had to succeed.

"I'm still trying to get reacquainted with her. Lady Eugenie is quite astute, and I feel if I move too quickly, she's going to suspect something."

"She already does," Brandon said with a snort. He took a sip of port. "I've made it quite clear to her that if she doesn't make a suitable match, I will do it for her."

"Woo her like you would any other young lady, Trent. That can't be too hard. Take her for a turn in the garden when we rejoin the ladies, send her flowers. Let her know you're interested. Women love being doted upon," his father suggested.

"I had already intended to suggest a turn in the gardens, my lord."

"Good. Make it so, my boy. There's much at stake here for all of us."

What exactly was at stake the two fathers had not been clear on. The railway access was important, but couldn't they do that separately? No, there was something else the two older men were still withholding, and he intended to find out what that was.

"I asked her if she'll be in attendance at the Duke of Hampshire's ball. I'll be sure to ask for two dances."

"Make sure one of them is a waltz," his father said stoically.

"I shall, oh, and sir, imagine my surprise when I learned from Lady Eugenie that you and Mother had postponed your holiday. When were you going to tell me?"

Trent knew he was treading on a sensitive subject. No one confronted the Duke of Marlborough. Not even his own son.

He waited for his father's reply.

"It was just decided this evening. Obviously, a holiday can wait. The betrothal and subsequent marriage of my heir is far more important than Paris."

"I imagine Mother wasn't happy?"

Marlborough frowned. "Your mother does as she is told with few questions asked. She knows the future lies in you and Lady Eugenie marrying."

"The latter I'm supposed to make happen. What if she refuses my affections? Or makes it more difficult than it should be. She already feels something is amiss around her and that she's being left out. Of what, she doesn't know."

"In that case, the marriage will be arranged, the date chosen for the two of you to marry," Brandon replied. "My daughter is headstrong, but if need be, I'll be forced to rein her in."

Trent nodded and finished off his port. He wasn't a

fan of cigars and wondered if he would be once he was older or inherited the dukedom. Not something he wanted, at least not now. His father still had many good years left.

He listened to the two older men discuss some bill trying to get through Parliament. Politics always fascinated him. How people fit into the grand scheme of their respective parties. Some day he would have his turn to try and turn things for the better, but for now, he was simply satisfied to listen to those who served tell their tales.

"Shall we rejoin the ladies?" Brandon asked finally.

"Yes," Marlborough replied. "And Trent here can ask Lady Eugenie to take a turn in the gardens."

Trent nodded in agreement and rose to follow them back to the drawing room. Whatever was at stake here, whatever the real reason for the two fathers to push marriage off on their children, he would find out what it was. He'd make discreet inquiries, of course, but he'd get to the bottom of it all. Though he knew it was for the good of the families for them to unite, he, too, felt as though there was something, something between the two older men, and he intended to find out exactly what it was. What they weren't telling him.

CHAPTER 3

Trent arose and was dressed early the following morning. He'd never been one to lie about in bed, even after a night of drinking and debauchery with his friends. Usually, he enjoyed an early morning ride if he were in the country, but since he was in London, schedules were a lot less lenient. Members of the nobility were rarely seen in the park at this hour of the day. Most who enjoyed Hyde Park at this hour were nannies with their charges.

Unfortunately, today it was raining, the sort of rain that had no intention of letting up any time soon. Pelting rain that kept most indoors. Instead, he would go downstairs to the breakfast room and enjoy reading his newspapers while he dined.

Before he went, he went in search of his valet, Miles, who was in the dressing room, putting away various articles of clothing. Neat and tidy he was.

"I need to have flowers sent to Lady Eugenie," he said. He stuck out his hand, which held a note he'd penned earlier. "See this is included, will you?"

"Yes, my lord. Any flower preference?"

He thought for a moment. "Roses. Pink roses, at least two dozen."

"Am I correct in thinking that my lord is going to court Lady Eugenie?"

Trent nodded. Was he that obvious? "Yes, though I don't imagine she's going to be a typical woman to court. She's quite headstrong, has her own opinions, and doesn't mind in the least to convey them."

"May I be so bold as to make a suggestion, my lord?"

"That's never stopped you in the past," he replied. "What is it?"

"Lady Eugenie is obviously going to have a good many suitors as the season starts. May I suggest you have flowers or some other sort of token delivered to her every morning?"

Trent grinned. "Excellent idea, Miles. Yes, you're right. Flowers today and tomorrow. I'll pen a note for tomorrow's. Thursday is the Hampshire ball. Perhaps I can find her a book. I'll leave you to making sure the flowers arrive at Lady Eugenie's."

"Yes, my lord. Anything else?"

Trent shook his head. "No, not now. I'm going to have breakfast, then I suppose I'll be forced to see to my correspondence."

The valet nodded and left the room. Miles would make sure the flowers were the freshest and that they were delivered promptly.

He proceeded downstairs to the breakfast room. As it was just him having breakfast, he usually had cook prepare it upon his arrival downstairs. Thus, he had time to glance over the newspapers for anything important while his breakfast was being made.

Trent was frugal that way. He saw no need in wasting food, even if he'd set it up for his staff to dine or share with their families any leftovers he might have. He tried to follow his father in that respect. Take care of your staff, and they'll take care of you, he always said.

He imagined Lady Eugenie was still abed on a day like today. His note had indicated he would call on her at two. If he was going to win her over, he needed to start immediately. He certainly didn't want their fathers to take matters into their own hands. He would be sure to stop and purchase her something else on the way. He wouldn't arrive empty-handed, and hopefully he'd make a favorable impression on her.

Tomorrow, he was certain, she and every other young lady would be preparing for the Hampshire ball. It was one of the finest held every season, and it was a major accomplishment to receive an invitation to the duke and duchess's residence.

He put down the newspaper he'd been staring blankly at as he heard the footman enter the room. The young man placed a plate before him with coddled eggs, ham, and some freshly made toast. He nodded at the footman and filled his fork with a piece of ham.

He tried to recall who might be invited to the Hampshire ball. There would be plenty of young ladies there, many in their first season. He would try to dance with a couple of them but pay Lady Eugenie the most attention.

Trent glanced out the window at the non-relenting rain. Nothing to do today but catch up on correspondence and accounts. The day was fit for neither man nor beast, then again, if he had to go out, it wouldn't be too chilly. At least he hoped when it came time to call on Lady Eugenie, the day will have warmed and make it more pleasant. As pleasant as a rainy day would allow.

He sat back in his chair and thought back to the last summer he'd spent at home before returning to Cambridge in the autumn. How many years had that been since his last year at university? Four? In any event, that summer had been memorable, though a bit faded now from time.

Lady Eugenie and he spent time riding across both estates that summer as they usually did, though that particular summer the time they'd spent together was far more than in previous years.

She always rode with a groom, as was her father's wish, but managed to outride whomever he sent with her. They would meet most of the time in secret, at a designated spot, and the two of them would ride in the opposite direction.

Usually they rode, some days they headed for a secluded spot in the river that ran through the two estates to sit and talk for hours without fear of being found.

At least it started out as sitting and talking. They'd discovered the attraction between them that had been building for years. One kiss led to another, even though Lady Eugenie made it quite clear she wasn't interested in marriage. No, she had other, more progressive plans for herself.

By then she'd had one season, and her father was becoming frustrated by the number of potential suitors she dismissed. Lady Eugenie was biding her time, telling him that she intended to go through the charade until her father gave in to her wishes.

Her wishes were simple, at least in her eyes. She wished to teach less fortunate children how to read and write, something this class would have less access to. She also knew her father and mother would be appalled by the notion.

Now here they were. Both her father and his wished them married to each other. Not only because it would make the families more powerful with such an alliance, but their fathers could pursue a joint business venture that would forever bind the two families.

Since that summer, life had taken them on separate paths, even though they'd promised each other to stay in touch until they could figure out a way to be together. Trouble was Lady Eugenie certainly seemed to have forgotten about their stolen times together. He would have to fix that. There was little time before the Hampshire ball, but even if he had to wait until then, he would remind Lady Eugenie of what they'd shared once. Perhaps once she remembered, she would soften her hard exterior and let him back in.

This wasn't something he shared with anyone, especially not his friends. They would be far too quick to judge and tease him about it, and he didn't need a hint of it getting back to Lady Eugenie, at least not from them.

Life certainly had a funny way of working.

LADY EUGENIE WAS SITTING in the morning room, listening to her mother go on and on about what it meant to be invited to the Hampshire ball, how she was to act, that she needed to find a suitable young man; the list went on and on. It wasn't as though she hadn't heard it all before. Her mother had a habit of doing this exact same thing every single social engagement they went to. Honestly, this wasn't her first season, though her mother acted as though it was.

The butler entered the room, directing a footman to place a very large vase full of pink roses on a nearby table. He handed her the card that had come with it.

She scanned the paper and smiled.

"Who are they from?" her mother trilled.

"The Marquess of Trent," she replied flatly.

"Oh my, they're gorgeous. I don't think I've seen three shades of pink together like this."

Eugenie neared the vase and bent to inhale the peppery fragrance. "Neither have I. I wondered how he remembered I liked roses, especially pink roses."

"Does it matter, my dear? What else does he say?"

"Only that he intends to call on me today, at two."

Her mother smiled like a cat who'd eaten a bird. "He certainly would be a catch, Genie."

She sighed. "I suppose he would." She wasn't interested, but her father was putting more pressure on her than ever to marry.

"Look at it this way, my dear; the two of you have known each other for years. You at least know him, his temperament, etc."

"It has been several years, Mother."

"True, but whose fault is that? When he has attended social events, you've avoided him. Why, I've never understood."

Eugenie tucked the card into her dress pocket. "Well, he's coming to call on me this afternoon."

"He is! Please don't run him off, my dear."

"I wouldn't dream of it," she replied. "If you'll excuse me, I need to find something appropriate to wear for when he calls."

"Yes, yes," the duchess urged. "You must look your best when the Marquess arrives."

Eugenie hurried upstairs to her rooms. She startled Babcock, who was putting away freshly ironed undergarments.

"The lavender muslin day dress, is it wearable or do you need to press it?"

"It won't take me long to ready it, my lady."

"Excellent. It seems the Marquess of Trent is going to call on me this afternoon, and I want to look perfect."

"You will be perfection, my lady," Babcock replied. "Let me take it below and get started on it."

"Thank you. I'm going to tend to some correspondence while I wait; otherwise, my mother's going to drive me crazy. You know how she is wanting me married."

She sat down at the small white writing desk placed in front of her windows. It had always been a favorite place to sit and peer down at the garden below. Especially on dreary, rainy days such as today.

Eugenie's mind wandered to Trent. What was he up to? After all this time, did he still retain feelings for her? Was he truly interested in courting her? Or was he trying to make some sort of mysterious male point that women weren't supposed to understand.

He did know her desire to open a school of some sort to teach less fortunate children how to read and write. They had spoken of it on more than one occasion, and he seemed to support her desire and need to pursue such a matter.

Would he have changed his mind after all this time? Had he turned into a younger version of his father? Neither her father nor his would ever understand a woman's need, or want, to do anything more than have children, be a gracious hostess for their husbands, and of course, be an obedient wife in the marriage bed. In other words, not to refuse him when he visited her chamber at night.

That was such an old-fashioned way of thinking. Women were not simply property to their husbands once they married. Couples should respect each other; the husband should be willing to allow his wife some latitude of compromise when it came to interests outside the home.

Eugenie continued to write her letter to her dear friend Olivia. She had recently married Viscount Grayson, and the two hadn't been writing as much as they once had. Eugenie hoped her friend was happy with her new husband. Theirs had been a whirlwind courtship, one even Eugenie hadn't seen coming. Her friend later confided in her that Grayson had compromised her, a child was now on the way, and the only solution was for them to marry and marry quickly.

She looked up at the rain pelting against the glass and smiled. Did Trent recall their stolen kisses, the intimacy of their stolen time together? Or was he like most men who would deny any of it happened? He had returned to university that autumn, and she never heard from him, except when he was home for the Christmas holiday, and even that had been strained. He was cordial when both their families got together as they usually did. He seemed almost aloof to her, like she was the young sister no one wanted to spend any time with.

Perhaps he did recall the time they spent together, at that place by the river which ran through both estates. The bend in the river where the trees made the perfect cover for a young couple to find some privacy.

She shook her head. Still, the season was just beginning. Her father had made it quite clear that he expected her to at least become betrothed this year, but should she wait and see what other young suitors she attracted, or should she be grateful someone as kind, someone who knew her so well was truly interested.

After all, the Earl of Derby had expressed an interest at a musical concert her parents had dragged her to when they'd first arrived. He'd sent chocolates and had taken her through Hyde Park in his landau. Nothing since then except a note telling her he had urgent business in Dover and would call on her upon his return.

She knew her mother had a day set aside for the two of them to visit her dressmaker for a last fitting on some gowns her mother had commissioned when they first arrived in London. She couldn't wait to see them.

The gown for the Hampshire ball had been the only one her mother had put a rush on, and Madame Marie was more than happy to oblige one of her best customers. The gown was a gorgeous confection of sapphire silk, her mother and Madame both agreeing she needed more color to make her hair and eyes stand out.

Finally finishing her letter, she turned to two others needing her attention. Her friend, Lady Harriet Worthington, had arrived in town with her parents and was wanting them to plan tea and shopping. Her father, too, had put his foot down about his daughter's lackluster interest in marriage. He expected Lady Harriett to become betrothed by the end of this season, or he would find a husband for her. Her father had little patience with his daughter's interest in wanting to write for a small women's paper. Proper young ladies weren't supposed to work outside the home in his opinion.

Men! Some were so ancient in their thinking, but a few, like Trent, were more willing to at least listen to a woman and even encourage her.

She put her thoughts aside and found a fresh sheet of paper and began to write Harriet. They needed to visit, and perhaps after the Hampshire ball, they could do just that. For this week, her mother had her busy, and then there was Trent's visit this afternoon. Would it turn into him calling more than just this one time?

It was best, she decided as she wrote Harriet, to keep him at a distance and see what he was all about. Intuition had taught her, where men were concerned, she shouldn't open her heart too fast. Trent had hurt her years ago when he returned to university, never writing her as promised. She had tried to put it off to the fact that he was finding his own way, and that his studies were far more important at the time. Still, why hadn't he written her after university?

"I've got your dress ready, my lady, if you're ready to change," she heard her maid say in the background.

"Yes, let me finish putting my thoughts in this letter, and I'll be right with you."

Quickly she finished what she had been saying to Harriet. She readied the letter and laid it with the other to give to the butler to post.

Now what she needed to do was clear her thoughts, think nothing but positive, happy ones, and find out what Lord Trent was all about.

CHAPTER 4

*E*ugenie sat near the fire watching her mother pretend to be busy with her needlework. She was there to be on hand when Lord Trent came to call. Oh, she would make small talk, then discreetly leave the two of them alone, with the drawing room door open of course.

The rain had not relented all day, so Eugenie was prepared that Trent might be late. Nothing moved in London, and it could even be worse with weather like this. It was slippery and dangerous on the cobblestone streets for horses. It always was. London was always in some sort of hurried frenzy, but add to it the rain, and it could spell disaster.

"He'll be here, my dear. He's not late anyway," the duchess murmured.

"I know that."

About that time there was a knock on the drawing room door, and the butler entered to announce the Marquess of Trent. He appeared in the room, tall and commanding. He approached both her and her mother.

He bent over the duchess's hand and murmured something before doing the same with her.

"Thank you for the flowers, my lord. They're beautiful," she said, looking straight at him rather than acting demure like her mother had instructed her to. Men prefer women who are subservient, her mother had said. Eugenie had no intention of starting a courtship with Trent being beneath him. Best for him to know they were on equal ground from the start.

"My pleasure," he replied. "I'm happy they pleased you."

Her mother immediately ordered tea before excusing herself from the drawing room. She arched her brow at Eugenie before turning to leave, as though telling her not to make a muck of this one.

"Come, sit, my lord," she said. "Dreadful day, isn't it?"

"It is," he agreed. He sat down in a chair near hers. He carried with him a package of some sort. Remembering he had it in his hand, he offered it to her. "I thought you might enjoy this."

She accepted the carefully wrapped item and began to open it. Inside she found a book on the sonnets of Shakespeare. He remembered they were among her favorite things to read. "Thank you, my lord. I'll treasure it always."

He sat back in the gold damask chair, the edges of his mouth curling up. "You're most welcome. I thought perhaps you might care to read one or two since it is too dreadful outside for a drive or walk today."

The butler and a footman reappeared with tea. The tray was placed on the table in front of Eugenie. She immediately began preparing two cups.

"I would be honored, my lord."

He accepted a cup from her. "Are you looking forward to the Hampshire ball?"

"Yes and no. Yes, because it's one of the grandest of the season, and no because I really do dislike social events like this. I could find other, more enlightening things to occupy my time other than dancing and flirting."

She watched him with amusement as he nearly spit his tea back into the cup. "Flirting?"

"Yes, every woman does it. Every unattached young woman is there for one thing and one thing only."

"And pray tell what would that be?"

"Why to land a husband, of course. Don't tell me you men aren't there in part to do the exact same thing. That is, if you're single. You attend balls, especially if you're on the marriage mart."

"No, you are right of course," he murmured. "What other sorts of things would you rather do than attend a ball?"

"Read or if I had the company of another, a good discussion would be welcome. And you?"

"I agree, a good book, perhaps a game of chess, and conversation with another."

She smiled, knowing the answer before she'd even asked, but she had to. "You play chess, my lord? Are you any good?"

"You know I play chess, and I'd venture to say I'm an average player."

She took a thoughtful sip of tea before setting the cup back on the tray. "Tell me something, my lord. Are you here on your own, because you wish to perhaps court me, or are you here at the whim of our fathers, who would love to see us married?"

He sputtered and put his cup on the table next to him. "I am here on my own bidding. Seeing you at dinner brought a lot of fond memories racing back."

She noted a faint smile cross his lips. "You haven't answered the second part of my question, my lord."

"Enough with the 'my lord', Eugenie. We're far beyond formalities. Or at least I thought we were."

"Very well, you were saying. . .Trent?"

He shook his head. "I am well aware that there is nothing more that our fathers would like than for us to marry."

"Very well, as long as you're being forthright with me."

"Shall I speak with your father?" he asked, his deep blue eyes piercing through her like a spear.

"Why don't we wait until after the Hampshire ball? Let's keep all of them wondering, shall we?"

He arched a brow. "I never thought you enjoyed playing games."

"I don't, but this is different. It's our lives that are at stake here. Our future."

"I agree, but you're playing with fire. I'm afraid if we don't act on our own, our fathers will act for us."

"Oh, I'm quite sure they will. I'm sure they have been plotting all along about how they could get us together. I'm simply not ready to let them have their way."

"Then we're in agreement. After the Hampshire ball, I'll speak with your father and get his permission to call on you."

"Yes, but understand this, Trent. I'm in no hurry to marry and be tied to one man. I have my own plans. I want to teach less fortunate children how to read and write. After a year or two of doing that, I may be willing to marry. First I will have my turn to contribute to something I believe in."

Trent smiled. "You are far more socially minded than anyone gives you credit for."

"I'm not my mother. I pay attention to what's going on around me, beyond the social events to the real world."

"You don't feel social functions are real world?"

She shook her head. "There is a world beyond the gossip and such. You know that as well as I do."

He glanced at the clock on the mantel. "As much as I

would love to listen to you read, I don't think I should overstay my visit."

"Perhaps next time?"

He rose from his chair. She followed his lead. "Thank you, my lord, for the book and visit. I shall look forward to seeing you at the ball."

Trent bent over her hand and kissed the back. "Until then."

Eugenie knew her mother was hovering either right outside the door or close by. Trent evidently was aware of the same thing. The blasted rules of polite society. It was all so phony. She found herself watching him leave, and as he did, she began to miss the summers they'd spent together.

The duchess glided across the room, picking up the book of sonnets Trent had brought her. "Shakespeare. How did he know?"

"Please, Mama, you know good and well Trent and I aren't strangers. He remembered from one of our many conversations we had over the summers."

"Yes, yes, I know. What did he say? Is he interested?"

"Of course he's interested, Mama. We'll see what transpires. He's also very astute to the fact that you and Papa and his parents would love nothing more than for us to wed."

"You believe he will propose?" the duchess trilled.

"Perhaps. If, and I say if, he does, it will be a long, long courtship. We both have things we would like to accomplish before marriage. It's something we agree upon."

"What could you possibly want to accomplish outside of marriage and giving your husband an heir? Any of your silly notions can be accomplished once you become marchioness."

Eugenie knew there was no reason to correct her

mother or convince her otherwise. As long as she and Trent were in agreement, that was all that mattered.

"Nothing, Mama," she said with a sigh. "But one social call does not mean there's a wedding to plan."

"Oh, there will be," the duchess said coyly. "There are things that are out of our hands. You'll see; everything will come together."

Eugenie sat back down and picked up the book Trent had brought. She couldn't believe she and Trent had actually spoken about a future together. In the past, well in the past, they had been younger with so much of the future still to come. They'd made promises to each other, but with the passing of time and life itself these faded.

But before she settled on one man, Eugenie wanted to see who else was out there. She had no expectations she could do better than Trent, but she also knew there would be others interested in garnering her affections. At least she hoped there were. In any case, she would play the game because once Trent spoke with her father, she would be off the market, and life might forever begin to change, and the last thing she intended to do was marry—not unless it was under her terms.

TRENT SAT BACK against the squabs as he returned home from calling on Lady Eugenie. The rain hadn't changed all day, and the afternoon had grown cooler because of it. He began to recall his conversation with her as he stared out the window of his carriage at the gray sky and virtually empty streets, all but void of pedestrian traffic.

It had gone too well—too easy. She had agreed to everything far too quickly, asking little in return. Her main concern had been a long courtship so she could pursue a dream of hers to teach less fortunate children to read and write. Something she could do as a married woman. He had no problem with that. He would even go so far as to help her establish such a school at his country home in Gloucestershire.

He knew her mother, the duchess, had been hovering near the open door, so the conversation he and Lady Eugenie had was superficial and muffled so the duchess wouldn't be able to make out what they were discussing.

Still, he was curious about her behavior. The young woman he knew would have questioned him more about his sudden interest and intentions. He thought he'd deflected her questions well enough, and she seemed convinced by his answers.

He was going to have to put together a plan. The sooner the better because he knew the outcome if he allowed her to dally too long. Their fathers would insist on an arranged marriage, and Lady Eugenie would certainly dig her heels in if it came to that, and it wouldn't matter if she were of age. She was still living under her father's roof and was considered under his protection until such time as she married. She would have no say in an arranged marriage. If it came to that, he wasn't sure what their relationship would be. Certainly not the lighthearted one they had always enjoyed.

He kept telling himself he was only doing this for the good and future of his family as well as Lady Eugenie's. For the two families to merge some of their business interests on their neighboring estates would mean jobs for villagers and would therefore help those less fortunate as his father, as well as Lady Eugenie's, provided not only for the nearby communities, but England as well.

The carriage came to a halt in front of Trent House, and he opened the door and quickly descended. He dashed up the steps to the open front door, where he handed his hat and gloves to a waiting butler.

"The duke is waiting in your study, my lord," the butler said dryly with a nod.

Trent shook his head. Was his father here to find out the sordid details of his afternoon visit to Lady Eugenie, or was there another reason which brought him out on this horrid, dreary, wet day?

The duke was sitting in front of Trent's desk, a glass of whiskey in his hand. He glanced up upon hearing Trent enter.

"I'm surprised to see you here on such a wet and dreary afternoon," Trent said casually. He poured himself two fingers of whiskey before sitting behind his desk, across from his father.

"Word reached me that you were paying a call on the Lady Eugenie. I merely thought I'd stop by and see how things are progressing if they're progressing. Was she agreeable?"

Trent sipped his whiskey and considered how to respond to his father. "Agreeable? To what? I merely paid her a call after sending her roses. I took her a book and we had a conversation."

"You know what I mean," the duke growled.

"The idea of my wishing to court her and speaking with her father for permission was one of the topics we discussed. She seems amenable, on the grounds I wait until after the Hampshire ball."

"It's a start. Anything else I should know about?"

"Only that she does not intend to be pressured into marriage by me or anyone else," he replied. "She is also aware of the fact that her father could arrange a marriage for her even now."

"She will heel; her father will see to that. You proceed as you've planned. I expect to be apprised of developments."

"Father, this is my future we're playing with here. I would much rather start a marriage off right, with us both agreeable to it. I'm afraid being forced to marry, even me, will make my life a living hell."

"Marriages are a partnership. Nothing more. Each has their place and knows what is expected of themselves and the other. She will have little say once you've married the girl. My advice to you is to tame Lady Eugenie. Get her with child as soon as possible."

"My concern right now is her agreeing to what we spoke of. I plan to call on her father and get his permission to court her. Then things can move along as planned."

"You need to hurry it along, get her to marry you. Without delay," the duke grumbled. taking a long sip of whiskey. "Compromise her; that way she'll have no choice but to agree to a quick wedding."

Trent said nothing as he peered at his father over the edge of his glass. Something felt off here. Or perhaps it was just him. His father had always been known to make things appear more dire than they actually were. His sister, Caroline, was a perfect example. Whatever it was, he wasn't about to give in to his father's demands to compromise Lady Eugenie. He had more integrity than that.

"I believe I'm capable of handling Lady Eugenie. Let me get her to agree to my seeking permission from her father for us to court. I'll take it from there." No sense telling his father everything, he'd find out on his own if he so chose.

The duke nodded. "Very well. Just don't take too long."

Trent nodded and finished his whiskey. "Anything else? Look, I know you and Lord Brandon aren't telling me everything as to why this marriage is so important. I want to know exactly what it is you're planning,"

"You've always had an overactive imagination."

"That's your answer? That I'm imagining what it is the two of you are plotting? You two have always been thick as thieves."

"I will tell you one more time. Convince Lady Eugenie to allow you to call on her. That's a start. Woo her, spend time with her, take her places, convince her. . .that shouldn't be hard. You've always done quite well where the ladies are concerned. Do it and do it fast, or else Lord Brandon and I will be forced to take matters into our own hands."

"I will do so, but I will not arouse her suspicions any more than they already are," he replied. He finished off his whiskey and placed the glass down on the desk in front of him.

His father rose. "Good, as long as we understand each other."

Trent tapped back his growing anger at his father. His father had always had high expectations for his children, and he couldn't fault his sister for acting in the manner in which she had. With him, it was different. He was his father's heir.

"Perfectly."

"Then I'll leave you. I imagine your mother is expecting me at a reasonable hour so I can get ready for this evening's affair."

The duke nodded and walked out the door. Trent hadn't said anything further, seeing there was nothing left to be said. His father had come to accomplish what he'd set out to do. To try and intimidate him.

Trent still had no firm answers as to what the two older men were really about. Yes, with a marriage between the two of them, it would make both families stronger. That shouldn't have a thing to do with a business venture, should it? There was no reason to his knowledge that they couldn't go on with or without him and Lady Eugenie being wed.

He needed to look further into the matter. Discreetly of course. He could make some inquiries or have someone do it on his behalf. The last thing he wanted to do was arouse the two dukes' suspicions.

Suddenly, his life had become far more complicated than it had been a few weeks ago. The unfortunate thing was who could he trust to assist him in finding things out. He stared down at the never-ending stack of correspondence. Now would be the perfect time to sort through it. It would keep his mind occupied and off of this madness.

He sat back down and poured himself another whiskey before going through everything. Invitations in one stack, bills in another, and correspondence in another. His mind, however, kept wandering back to the Lady Eugenie.

CHAPTER 5

*H*ampshire House was a massive structure looming out of the London streets. It sat on a corner lot, far larger than most. Windows were aglow with candles, warmly greeting guests as they descended their carriages.

A butler stood at the top of the steps, a massive door open, leading into a cavernous hall hung with portraits and tapestries. An imposing marble and stone staircase curved up to the second floor, the grand hall lit by a massive crystal chandelier.

Hats and gloves were taken by servants who welcomed them and escorted them to the staircase, where they were informed the duke and duchess would receive them.

Lady Eugenie dutifully followed her parents, immediately recalling their guests having attended several of her own parents' social events.

The duke was clad in tailored evening clothes and moved with confidence. He was a striking man, and his expression was reserved. It was obvious who he was by his powerful presence.

His wife stood beside him wearing a magnificent flowing ball gown in red silk. The gown was obviously

43

made in Paris, or the duchess had a modiste who knew French fashion in great detail.

"Lady Eugenie, welcome." The words tumbled out of the duchess's mouth like honey.

Eugenie curtsied as she stared into gingerbread-colored eyes. "Your Grace, your home is lovely."

The duchess was a slender, tall woman with hair the color of dark chocolate, and fine features. She radiated the same aloof demeanor that her husband displayed. "Thank you, and once again welcome, Lady Eugenie."

She followed her parents as they led her into the ballroom, which was breathtakingly beautiful. Garlands of white flowers decorated the room, with gold ribbon running through. At this point, her father and mother separated, her father joining a group of men he obviously knew, and her mother staying with her. The duchess led them to where the Countess of Bath was standing with two other women engaged in a lively conversation.

Her mother quickly introduced her to the ladies before looking out at the ballroom. Eugenie knew what she was doing. Scanning the room for possible dance partners for her daughter, the marquess of Trent to be exact. It was, after all, a well-orchestrated dance in itself. All the players knew their parts and acted their best performance.

Out of nowhere, Trent appeared. He made a fuss over the older women, paying them each careful attention. Of course he would; each woman's husband was or had the potential to be a business associate or friend of the marquess.

He stood in front of her, taking her gloved hand in his. He bent over and kissed the back "Lady Eugenie, you look exquisite this evening. Might I sign your dance card?"

Eugenie tried to keep from smiling at his effort. He

was trying hard to conform to the expectations and ways of the ton, but it was obvious to her that social events such as this ball were uncomfortable to him.

She handed him the card and pencil. "Certainly, my lord."

"I was hoping for two dances, my lady? The supper set and perhaps a waltz afterwards?"

She nodded, aware of his blue eyes gazing at her. "I look forward to them."

Eugenie watched him closely as he penciled in his choices. He was dressed similarly to the other gentlemen. His dark hair curled over the starched white collar of his shirt. The black suit he wore made him almost look exotic.

He passed the card and pencil back to her. "Lady Eugenie, if you'll excuse me," he murmured.

"Again, I look forward to our dance, my lord." She curtsied and watched him as he bowed, turned, and left her presence. Eugenie was acutely aware they were expected to be seen together tonight. Lord Trent had requested two dances, which in the eyes of all signaled he was interested.

Unfortunately, her mother had decided to keep her on a short leash this evening, denying her request to visit with her good friend, Lady Helena, who was standing across the ballroom with a couple of other young women she was not familiar with. Her mother stood close by with two matronly older women. One she recognized as Lady Charlotte Tolbert, viscountess Brown.

She shrugged her shoulders, the two knowing they'd see each other a bit later, after their mothers tired of keeping such a close eye on them. Their mothers were also aware of the mischief they could cause together, neither woman believing it was healthy for their daughters to spend time at any gathering. She and Lady Helena had already made plans on how to sneak past the prying eyes of their mothers. Tonight was a night to be savored; to be part of something as exclusive as the Hampshire ball was truly a coup.

Until then, she would pacify her mother and act as though what the older women were discussing was of importance to her.

By the time Trent came to lead her out on the dance floor for the supper set, Eugenie had only danced twice, both young men boring and without merit in her eyes. Trent, on the other hand, knew how to say all the right things, and he proved it once again.

"Lady Eugenie, I believe this is our dance?"

"It is, my lord," she muttered and walked onto the dance floor with him.

They took their places. "Don't look, but it seems we've become very interesting. Our parents are all on the perimeter watching our every move," he whispered as the dance began. It was a quadrille, so perhaps they would all bore and return to whatever they'd been in the midst of before the dance began.

Trent said little as they went through the motions. The quadrille left little time for a serious conversation. Even by the time the dance was finished, Eugenie noted their fathers still standing at the edge of the dance floor, their heads together in some sort of private conversation.

"Come," he said in a low voice, "would you care to get some air on the terrace?"

"Yes, that would be nice," she replied.

He led her to the open French doors that led to the terrace. They were far from alone, as other couples walked, and a few engaged in conversation. Even a few were walking along a torch lit path through the gardens. The evening was perfect, and being here, it was hard to imagine one was in the middle of London and not some country estate.

Trent led her to the balustrade where they looked out over the garden below. They stood there for a moment, saying nothing. Finally, Trent broke the silence.

"You look exceptionally lovely this evening, Eugenie."

She gazed up at him and moistened her lips before responding. "Thank you."

"I know you're aware of the expectations our parents have of us this evening."

"Yes, and I really don't care," she murmured.

He cocked a brow. "And that's going to prove a problem."

"Why?"

"You know why. They have high expectations we marry."

She shook her head. "We've been over this before. You know how I feel on the matter."

"I do, but Eugenie, we might not have a choice in the matter."

She said nothing for a moment. "They wouldn't dare!"

"I had a visit from my father, who made it very clear what was expected of me, at whatever cost."

She cocked her head. Trent could almost see the wheels spinning inside her head. "Is there something you're not telling me because I've been over and over this scenario in my head a dozen times. There is no reason why a marriage between us would financially help either family. Our fathers can go about whatever it is they're about, make money without us being made pawns."

"I also have tried to figure out what they're up to. Think hard, Eugenie. I've got a man looking into the matter, but I'm not sure he'll find anything in time."

"In time for what? What aren't you telling me, Trent?" Surprisingly, she didn't look overly panicked. Instead, Eugenie looked like a lioness on the prowl.

"I'm not sure. Only that I'm being pressured to get you to agree to a marriage, any way I can."

One side of her mouth curved up. "Or they'll make it an arranged marriage. I know."

They stood there in silence. "Come, I should take you back inside. It's time to eat, and I'm sure we're being looked for."

"Let them."

"Would you care to accompany me to the buffet?" he asked with a wink.

"Yes, I believe I would."

They walked back through the French doors to join others at the buffet. He handed her a plate, and silently they made their choices of which there were many. Both sets of parents hovered nearby. The two duchesses pretended to be interested in the buffet while the dukes appeared to be in deep conversation about something important.

"Come," Eugenie hissed to him in a low voice.. "Let's act as though we're enjoying a meal together."

"That's what we're doing, Eugenie," he said with a sigh..

"But I think I may have figured out what our fathers are about."

"Why didn't you say so?"

Eugenie shook her head, walking toward what was supposed to be an orange grove. There were chairs nearby, and she led them to a pair.

They hadn't even settled with their dinner; Trent was too impatient to know what she'd thought of. "Are you going to tell me or not?"

"I don't know why I didn't think of this before."

"What, what?"

"My grandfather left me a rather large parcel of land near where they are working. When I marry, it of course reverts to my husband. I believe should my husband die prematurely I am to be given fair market value for the land from my family. Which we know will be a pittance of what it's worth."

Trent arched a brow. "That would explain a lot. Our fathers can't proceed without it, and in order to do so, you must marry me because they expect I'll give the go ahead for them to use the land."

"Thus, an arranged marriage if you can't convince me to marry you."

"Exactly."

"What are we going to do, Trent?" Eugenie looked amused. "There is no other way out of this unless I were to run off and marry another man, but there is no one else."

"So what are you suggesting? I know you have a plan."

"Not so much a plan, but a way to stall things until we can be sure this is what's going on, or you can find out from your solicitor if we have any options."

"I'm listening," he muttered.

"You go to my father and get his blessing to court me. We can go through the motions while you research the matter."

"That sounds like the logical solution."

"Then at least that's settled. Call on me tomorrow and take me riding. We can discuss the matter through and with more privacy."

"Very well," he replied. "I'm afraid it's all we've got for the moment, and I'm sure you can make everyone believe you're thrilled we're courting."

"I can," she said triumphantly. She placed a gloved hand on his arm. "Not to say I won't enjoy spending time with you, Trent. I will, but we have a mission, and time will quickly run out if we can't figure this all out."

"I agree with you. Our fathers won't sit by while we enjoy a lengthy courtship. They've made that abundantly clear."

"Then let's give them a show, shall we?"

TRENT FOUND his gaze wandering to the dance floor, looking for Lady Eugenie. She had gone from where he'd left her after enjoying a meal—in her mother's care. Not that she needed to be in anyone's care; it was the way things were done. He'd lost track of her, but had seen her twirl nearby in the arms of the Duke of Northshire.

A twinge of jealousy ran through him. Ridiculous, he told himself as his eyes scoured the ballroom and found the pair. Lady Eugenie was laughing at something Northshire had said.

"They make a handsome couple, don't you think?" Preston snickered as he stood next to Trent.

Trent pretended he had no idea who his friend was referring to. "Who?"

"You know exactly who I'm talking about. Northshire and Lady Eugenie. You've been standing here looking for her ever since he took her to the dance floor."

"Don't be ridiculous," Trent snapped.

Preston threw back his head and laughed. "Keep telling yourself that, my friend. Don't deny it; you're quite attracted to the lady."

Trent sighed. "What if I am? What of it?"

"According to your father, a match between the two of you is imminent."

His head swung around to his friend. "My father said that? You heard him?"

"Yes, he was talking to Lord Bailey and Lord Phillips. He was bragging about the match."

An idea came to mind. Preston's brother, Tristan, and cousin, William Fitzsimons, were solicitors and partners in a firm his cousin had inherited from his father. Perhaps he could hire them to look into this matter of Lady Eugenie's land.

"Do you think I could hire your brother to look into a matter for me? Something quite personal?"

Preston nodded. "I'm sure he would. I'll send a note around in the morning and tell him to be expecting to hear from you. Is there a reason you can't make the same inquiry through your own solicitor?"

"Yes. I don't want word getting back to my father."

"Say no more," Preston agreed. "I'll make mention to my brother that's it's a delicate matter you wish to discuss with him."

"Thank you. I'm sorry I can't be more forthcoming about it, but until I get the details sorted, it's best left that way."

"You'll tell me when you're ready." He motioned to where the dance was coming to an end. "You may have competition. Lord Northshire seems quite interested in Lady Eugenie."

"Who said I'm interested? As for Northshire, he's too old for her, and he may be charming, but Lady Eugenie can see right through that."

Preston cocked a brow, smiling. "The duke isn't but a few years older than we are, and what he lacks in looks, he certainly makes up in charm."

"She would be miserable with him. His wife died, leaving him with no heir, which is precisely why he's on the marriage mart."

The pair watched as Northshire returned Lady Eugenie to her mother. Once he left them, he strode across the room and passed near them, heading to one of the card rooms the Duke of Hampshire had set up for his gentlemen guests. Northshire made sure Trent was looking; a smirk pasted on his face as he passed them.

"You don't think he'll seek out Lady Eugenie's father, do you?" Preston murmured.

"This is not the time or place to be asking a young lady's father's permission to call on his daughter. It just isn't done."

"True, but there's nothing that says he can't get to know the man better, form an alliance, let Brandon know his interest in his daughter."

"Why don't you keep a discreet eye on him. I have a waltz with Lady Eugenie."

Preston bent his head. "Don't make mention of Northshire. Just enjoy her company."

"Spoken like a true lady's man," Trent replied and began walking toward Lady Eugenie to claim his dance with her.

He led her to the dance floor and gathered her in his arms. A waltz was considered a more intimate dance since couples touched more than other dances. "Are you enjoying yourself?"

She flashed him a smile. "Do you mean the entire evening or just now, in this moment?"

"As I know how you feel about being here and your every move scrutinized, why don't you tell me what you're feeling this moment."

"At ease. At this moment, I feel completely at ease," she whispered. "I'm sure you saw the duke and me dancing, and before you ask. He's the sort of man I'd never want to be with."

"How's that?" It wasn't a complicated question; he indeed wanted to know. How else could he learn what she might be feeling. It had, after all, been four or five years since they'd spent time together. A long time some would say.

"He's the sort of man who views women as possessions. He believes when a man marries, his bride immediately becomes his property."

He nodded. "I would have to agree with you."

She smiled up at him. Eugenie felt so right in his arms. Like they were meant to be together, but he'd thought that the last summer they'd spent together.

"Come," he said. "Let's not talk of the duke or any other outsiders. Let's enjoy the moment, just you and me."

"Let's," she replied.

The couples swirled by, themselves included. Anyone watching from the side was now a blur, and there was no one else present except the two of them. He wanted the waltz to last forever, to never end. Trent, at that moment, had no idea how he might breathe or even survive if she truly decided they weren't suited for each other.

Time would tell once he had her father's approval to call on his daughter. In that moment, he knew he had the one, the mother of his children right in his grasp. Failure was not an option. He must convince her that her future lay with him.

CHAPTER 6

rent arrived at the Duke and Duchess of Brandon's townhouse the next afternoon to a stream of men coming and going. Those entering came with flowers and other gifts, all in an effort to win over Lady Eugenie. Obviously, she had made quite an impression on more than one young man.

Ignoring the hopeful, he by-passed the line and proceeded to the front door where a very patient butler nodded and let him enter. He found Lady Eugenie in the grand hall attired in a dark green riding outfit. She was talking to a young viscount, doing her best to pay attention to him, but when Trent's eyes locked with her deep blue eyes, she looked relieved.

She said something to the viscount before walking to where he stood.

"Lady Eugenie, you look well today. Are you ready to go for our ride?" he asked, a slight smile crossing his lips.

"Thank you, my lord. I've been looking forward to this." Her eyes sparkled with mischief.

"I brought a mare for you to ride. I think you'll like her." He offered his arm and led her past the waiting would-be suitors, down the stairs to where a groom stood with a black and white piebald mare.

Eugenie approached the animal quietly, stroking her nose and talking softly to her. Trent stood, waiting to assist her to mount the mare. Eugenie patted the mare's neck before stepping on the mounting block.

With Eugenie settled on the side saddle, he strode over to Solomon, his black stallion, and swung his leg over the animal's back. "Are you ready?"

"Yes," she replied, clucking to the mare to encourage her to walk.

They walked in silence until they were far enough from the Brandon house. He smiled. "You had quite the line of suitors today."

"You have no idea. Lord Northshire came to speak with my father. Luckily, Papa had a previous engagement and wasn't at home when he called."

"I was afraid he might do something like that. He's quite determined about finding a bride."

The entrance to the park neared, and Trent guided her past the crowds and onto a path where other riders were enjoying the warm afternoon sun.

"Thank you for rescuing me," she murmured.

"You obviously made quite an impression at the Hampshire ball."

"Yes, all the wrong ones, but my parents were quite pleased, or at least my mother seemed to be."

He glanced down at her. She was still an accomplished horsewoman, even if she did dislike sidesaddles. She hadn't made mention of that, but Trent knew she would remind him at some point. "You mentioned Northshire came to speak with your father?"

"Yes. He thought he could call on me in order to wait on my father, but his plan was thwarted by our butler. I'm afraid he's quite determined."

"Don't worry about Northshire."

She smiled. "You have a plan, my lord?"

"I do. I have someone looking into some things for me. I thought it easier if someone else made discreet inquiries on my behalf."

"I don't know how long I can hold my father off. He's quite determined for me to marry. You're the top contender as we both know."

"I know."

She stopped the mare. "I wish I were a man. I could simply leave until our fathers come to their senses."

"You mean run off?" he asked as he started walking Solomon once again. The stallion did not like standing in one spot for long, not when there was so much activity going on around him.

"Yes, I would have my own money, not the pin money I'm given monthly. Real money, enough to take me to the continent or Scotland. Somewhere away from our plotting fathers."

"I hadn't thought of that as an option."

She walked the mare briskly. "Unfortunately, I know of nowhere I could go without my father finding me and stopping me along the way. Plus, I have no funds."

"Eugenie, you know you can't run off. Your reputation would be ruined."

She nodded. "I know, but I can always dream." She clucked to the piebald. "Come, my lord, let's enjoy a brisk gallop. I believe your black beast would be very much appreciative."

"Stay close," he said, looking around the path in front of them. He urged Solomon into a slow gallop.

He shook his head as Lady Eugenie pushed her mare on, passing him. Nothing had changed; she still didn't follow instructions when it came to certain matters. This wasn't their country estates where they could run as fast and as far as they wished. This was London.

Trent caught up with her with little trouble. He blocked her from continuing down the path. "What did I just tell you? You aren't the only one out here. You know as well as I do there are rules to follow when riding in the park."

"You are so boring, Trent. You need to lighten up," she replied haughtily.

"Not when you blatantly disregard others. What if you'd lost control, or another horse came out of one of the adjoining paths and scared the mare? You'd be on the ground, hopefully uninjured."

He walked alongside of her, trying his best not to look at her for fear his feelings would take over. He was already seething at her willful act, afraid he might say something he would regret. He shook his head and continued to ride alongside her.

"If you want to gallop without a care, you need to come earlier in the morning before others rise."

"I'm sure one of my father's grooms would accompany me since I'm sure you would still be abed."

He stared at her in disbelief. "Why would you say such a thing. I rise at dawn, I'll have you know."

"Because you're an unattached man and a rake. I imagine your evenings are spent doing things you certainly won't discuss with me."

"You have an overactive imagination, Lady Eugenie."

She arched a brow and gazed at him. "Do I?"

He ignored her for a moment. "Come, we've been gone long enough. I must get you home."

She neared, walking the mare close, a gloved hand extending and covering his. "I have enjoyed this, Trent. Thank you for remembering my love of riding. . .even if I must ride in a blasted side saddle."

"You're most welcome. Perhaps next time I'll bring my landau."

"I would like that," she replied.

If nothing else, this afternoon had left him with an unsettling feeling and more.

EUGENIE ENTERED the drawing room after leaving Trent. She'd invited her best friend, Lady Helena. This was the first time the two had seen each other since the Hampshire Ball. Lady Helena had married the Earl of Dover, Thomas Conley. Eugenie envied her friend as she and the earl had found true love, something she was beginning to wonder if she might never have.

Helena stood upon seeing Eugenie, and the two friends embraced like two long lost sisters. Truth was Helena was the closest thing to a sister she had.

"Marriage agrees with you," Eugenie said, holding her friend off at arm's length. "You seem so...so happy."

Helena blushed. "I am, terribly. The earl is more than I imagined."

The door opened, and the butler appeared with a footman who held a tray bearing tea. He placed it on the table in front of Eugenie, and the two men retreated and left the room.

Eugenie began to prepare tea. "Are you in town long?"

"Yes, at least until the season ends. He has business affairs to attend to." She accepted the cup from Eugenie. "You have been riding? With whom? Tell me, I must know!"

Blushing, Eugenie stirred her tea before answering her dear friend. "Do you remember our neighbors in the country, the Duke of Marlborough?"

"Yes. I recall a scandal with the daughter, Lady Caroline, but scarcely recall her brother."

"Well, the Marquess of Trent and I used to ride every summer while growing up," she murmured. "Anyway, he's expressed an interest. That is who I was riding with today."

"You must tell me everything!" Helena gushed.

"I will, but first I want to hear about your wedding trip. How was it, and where did you go?"

Helena smiled broadly. "It was divine. We visited Paris and Vienna."

"Oh, I've always wanted to go to Vienna. Is it as grand as they say it is?"

"Grander," her friend replied. "With your love of music, you would be in heaven. You'd love the architecture as well."

"Did you get to attend many concerts while you were in Vienna?"

Helena nodded. "Yes, we went to three. There is so much musical history there with the composers. It is quite different from what one experiences in London."

"What about Paris?"

"Ah, Paris is Paris. The earl's family owns a home in a fashionable part of Paris. We were able to enjoy the city without feeling pressured to leave a hotel. If we wanted to stay in, we could. We weren't far from shops or the theaters."

"Sounds heavenly. I've only ever been with my mother and father."

"Perhaps you'll meet a wonderful man, and he'll take you to Paris for your wedding trip."

"First I need to find a husband."

"What of this marquess?" Helena teased.

Eugenie chose a small cake off one of the trays, and set it down on her empty plate. "It's much more complicated with the marquess."

"How so?"

"Our fathers are trying to force a marriage between us."

"Your father, arranging a marriage for you?"

"It could come to that if Trent and I do not become betrothed on our own," she replied quietly.

"But why?"

"That is what Trent is attempting to find out." Eugenie went on to explain to her friend what they did know right now.

"Could you stand being married to this man if it came to an arranged marriage?" Helena inquired.

"I suppose, but he also is aware of the fact I have no plans to be forced into doing anything I do not wish to do."

The look Helena had on her face was almost one of pity. "Eugenie, we are mere women. You know how society, meaning men, views us. We're their property."

"Only when we marry."

"Right now, you're under your father's protection. You won't have that forever."

"I want to be my own person, without a man dictating what I can and cannot do. I want to start a school somewhere and teach less fortunate children how to read and write."

Helena shook her head. "You still think of doing that? How? How are you going to fund it without a husband? Your father certainly won't do it."

All of a sudden, the drawing room door swung open, and Eugenie's mother, the duchess, swept into the room. Eugenie silently shuddered at the appearance of her mother. The duchess would do what she did best, take over a conversation.

"My dear Helena, how wonderful to see you," the duchess gushed. "You must tell us all about your wedding trip to the continent."

Eugenie tried not to roll her eyes. "Helena just finished telling me all about her visits to Paris and Vienna. I'm sure she doesn't want to repeat herself."

"Nonsense. I simply love Paris as you know, but Vienna is so filled with romance in its own unique way. Don't you think so?"

"Yes, it is," Helena replied. She picked up her tea cup and took a sip, her eyes locking with Eugenie's, pleading for help. "Eugenie was telling me about the marquess calling on her."

"Indeed, he is. There will be a wedding to plan soon. We're just waiting on Trent to offer for her."

"Which I explained to Helena wasn't going to be happening any time soon. The marquess respects my reasons for not wishing to marry at this time."

The duchess shook her head. "Eugenie has this silly notion she needs to teach less fortunate children how to read and write. Something she could oversee as a marchioness or even duchess when the time comes; don't you agree, Helena?"

The new countess chose her words carefully. "Eugenie is my best friend. I would hope she would marry for love as I did with the Earl. I think she should be allowed the chance to find a love match first."

"Her father grows impatient, I'm afraid. Sometimes family and duty are more important than love. Love can be found after a wedding if one chooses to do so. Look at her father and me. Ours was not a love match, but over the years, we've come to love and respect each other."

Helena, knowing she wasn't going to convince the duchess, grew quiet as she thought out her reply. "Eugenie will do what is right."

"She will; she was raised to put her feelings aside no matter how sentimental. The Duke of Northshire has approached her father about marriage."

"Northshire is a toad," Eugenie blurted out. "I'll never marry him."

"You'll do as you're told should the marquess not come around. And quickly."

"Trent will not be bullied. Not by Papa or his own father."

"Well, she did go riding with him today," Helena offered. "That's surely progress."

"It is. How was it, my dear?"

"Fine. It wasn't like in the country, but we were able to enjoy a leisurely ride."

The duchess poured herself a cup of tea and took a sip. "Has he declared his interest?"

"Mother!"

"Well, you know where your father stands on the matter."

To appease her mother, Eugenie gave in, letting the older woman hear what she wanted to hear. "We've discussed the matter. He's respectful I would like some time before we formalize it all."

Helena clapped her hands together. "A late summer wedding would be beautiful, Eugenie."

The Duchess of Brandon shook her head. "There will be no long, drawn-out betrothal. A wedding will happen as soon as the marquess has asked her father."

"You see," she addressed her friend. "This is exactly what I've had to go through. Our parents view this marriage as one to combine our two families."

"It's done all the time," the duchess snapped.

"Perhaps," Eugenie replied, "but it's not going to happen with me."

"You will have no choice in the matter if you and the marquess don't come to some sort of understanding."

"Mother, I'm sure Helena didn't come for tea to listen to us disagree. I, for one, want to hear more about the wedding trip and her new London residence."

"Dover residence is nowhere as grand as this. The earl's great-grandfather had it rebuilt after the original house burnt to the ground."

"I've been in it twice, both times when the late Earl

was still alive. It was replicated to the original structure if I'm not mistaken," Lady Brandon mused. She cut a piece of a delicate creme cake with her fork and took a mouthful.

"It was. The grand hall is one of the most beautiful I've seen with the priceless tapestries he brought back from his travels."

"I can't wait to see it," Eugenie said softly.

"Perhaps the countess and earl will invite you and Trent to dinner before the season is over," the duchess trilled.

"We will. Dover and I are planning to sit down and discuss social events we need to attend or have before we retire to the country," Helena agreed.

The duchess rose. "If you will both excuse me, I'm supposed to meet with cook about next week's menus. We normally take care of it in the morning, but things got delayed." She smiled at Helena. "It was so wonderful to see you, my dear. I would be most appreciative if you could help me to convince my daughter of her duties."

Helena smiled back. "I will try, Your Grace."

Eugenie gritted her teeth trying not to blurt out something to her mother, something her mother wouldn't want to hear, but she knew it would fall on deaf ears. Instead, she watched her mother quit the room.

Helena touched Eugenie's hand. "I see what you mean. You said the marquess has things under control?"

"Yes, he has an idea, but has men looking into it before he can share whatever it is with me."

"He would certainly be a more palatable match than the duke if it came down to it."

Eugenie sighed. "I suppose since no one is listening to me when I say I'm not interested in marriage at this time."

"Would it be so bad?"

"More than likely. Men change the moment they marry. We become their property and have no thoughts of our own."

"I'm not sure that is entirely true. The earl hasn't changed into an ogre."

Eugenie pursed her lips, shaking her head. "You're just married, just back your wedding trip. It's still new. Trust me, he'll change. They all do."

"Not always," Helena replied softly.

"Things will be different with us now, won't they? You're married. You'll be expected to socialize with the other matrons at the seasons' events."

"No, you know as well as I do it doesn't mean we give up our unmarried friends. If anything, we push them into a match."

Both young women laughed. While it might not be true for now, Eugenie knew as time went by, her best friend would be caught up in another world. One that their mothers were part of. And Eugenie—well, Eugenie would either marry or become a spinster, destined to sit along the perimeter of a dance floor, rarely being asked to dance. It was wrong in her eyes that society was so judgmental, but if she could have things her way, she would carry herself no differently than she did now. The hell with society rules. She needed to make her own contingency plans. Trent might not finish with his before their fathers pushed the issue.

"You seem a million miles away," Helena said.

"This entire matter has gotten out of hand, that's all. I must figure out a solution and soon."

"Do you really have a serious plan? Or might Lord Trent be a solid, reliable match?"

"You, too, Helena?"

"You've known him for years, and he seems genuinely concerned about you and this plot your fathers seem to be devising. If he's even mentioned marriage, why not give it consideration? It would be far better than that man sniffing around."

"I have considered Trent, and you're right, he would be a far more agreeable match than the alternative," Eugenie replied.

"Excellent! When will you see him again?"

"At the theater tonight. We've been invited to watch the play in the Duke of Marlborough's box. Lord Trent is supposed to be in attendance."

"Excellent."

"Perhaps, but we'll be under the watchful eye of both sets of parents," Eugenie said.

"And the marquess will be there to rescue you should some old aristocrat try and play for your affections."

Eugenie laughed lightly as she placed her tea cup back on the tray. "You've thought of everything, haven't you?"

"You need someone to look out after you. Someone of the same sex who's been through this recently."

"Perhaps you're right. I'd rather have you advise me than my mother."

"You, my dear Eugenie, know what you want; don't ever forget that," Helena said. She rose from her chair. "I'm afraid I must leave. Perhaps I'll see you this evening."

"Then you and the earl will be in attendance?"

She smiled shyly. "Yes. That is unless Lord Conley finds something else to keep us at home."

"Helena!"

"The marriage bed is so much better than I expected. Conley has been such a patient and gentle lover. You'll see. It doesn't have to be solely for the purpose of procreating."

"So I've heard."

Helena arched a brow. "Really? Where have you

heard details of the marriage bed? In one of your romance novels?"

"Not mine, my mother's! Haven't I told you I discovered where she hides her collection?"

"No, but from the look on your face, they are far more scandalous than what you normally read."

"Yes, and I can see why she hides them."

"You can tell me more later. The hour grows late."

Eugenie nodded. "It does. Hopefully, I'll see you both this evening."

She walked her friend out of the drawing room to the great hall grateful for having had this visit. Sometimes all it took was a fresh perspective on matters, and Helena never steered her wrong. She had been right about Archibald Smythe, second son of an obscure earl. While Archibald had been attentive in the beginning, once her father gave his permission for the courtship, Smythe turned into a possessive, hardened shell of himself. He yelled at Eugenie, put her down in front of others, and treated her like she was no better than a chamber maid.

Tired of the berating, Eugenie broke things off. Surprisingly, her father had agreed with her reasons. But that was before whatever scheme he and Trent's father had devised. Now two dukes were hellbent on their children marrying.

Helena was right on one thing. Trent was the lesser evil between him and the old man.

CHAPTER 7

*T*rent was standing to one side, speaking with a long-time friend of the family, Lord Timothy Mackenzie. They were engaged in a conversation about Trent joining Mackenzie's yearly summer hunting party on his Scottish estate.

Discreetly, he was able to find out his sister lived about a day's ride from the Mackenzie estate. His mind was racing with ideas. He and Eugenie had already discussed the possibility of her going to stay with his sister, though his idea went beyond Eugenie simply hiding there. His intention was to marry her.

He looked up as the duke and duchess entered; Lady Eugenie followed. She was wearing a dove gray and lavender colored gown. He felt himself pulled toward her. She was beautiful in so many ways.

Their eyes locked, and he politely excused himself from Mackenzie's company. "I need to greet guests, if you'll excuse me, Mackenzie. I am very interested in your hunting party and want to hear more."

"Aye, go greet the lass. You haven't been able to take your eyes off her since she walked in the room."

Trent nodded and walked over, greeting the duke

and duchess before turning his attention to Lady Eugenie.

"I enjoyed our ride, my lord."

"I'm glad. Did you like the mare I chose for you?" he asked.

"I did. You've trained her well."

He shifted his weight. He was uncomfortable with both sets of parents so close. Anything either of them said would be scrutinized by them, and he had much he still wished to speak with Eugenie about. Scotland for one, though here would make that harder.

"Would you like something to drink?" he asked. "I believe there's some lemonade."

She nodded. "Yes, I'm quite parched."

He led her over to the seats overlooking the box and onto the stage. "Wait here, and I'll get you a glass. Anything else?"

"No, thank you. I'll partake during intermission," she replied.

Trent went over to the refreshment table and waited while the footman poured a glass of lemonade. He heard a voice behind him, the Duke of Northshire. As he turned to look, the duke had already caught sight of Lady Eugenie and made his way to her side and had sat down next to her.

"Seems you have some serious competition in Northshire," his father said in a low voice as he stood at Trent's side.

"Lady Eugenie regards him as an old toad. She has no interest in him."

"Have you made any progress with her?"

He nodded. "I intend to speak with her father tomorrow."

"I'll mention that to him this evening. Just in case Northshire tries to do the same."

"Yes, well, I plan on speaking with the duke myself this evening to find out how early he receives callers."

His father clapped him on the shoulder. "Excellent. I'm glad to see you making progress with the young lady."

He nodded and walked over to Lady Eugenie. He gave her the glass of lemonade, being civil to Northshire and no more. As the duke had no intention of vacating his spot next to Lady Eugenie, Trent sat on the other side of her and listened as Northshire tried to dominate the conversation.

He'd written his sister explaining in detail what was transpiring and how neither of them wished to be forced to wed. Perhaps she would have some suggestions or guidance. When he'd written Caroline, he hadn't thought that might be one of the first places his father and hers might look.

What he needed was to be able to speak with Lady Eugenie without interruption. Northshire was making that extremely impossible.

He sat next to her the entire first half of the performance, gritting his teeth as the duke manipulated any conversation. When Trent did look in the older man's direction, he was met with a callous smirk.

When intermission came, he stood as Lady Eugenie excused herself. He thought nothing of it, instead joining a conversation their two fathers were having with Mackenzie about deer in Scotland.

No one noticed when Northshire silently slipped from the box.

Not until it was time for the performance to resume. The Duchess of Brandon was distressed that Lady Eugenie hadn't returned. Trent offered to escort the duchess to the closest retiring room where Lady Eugenie would have gone.

When Lady Brandon reappeared, she looked distressed. "Lady Eugenie was here, but that was ages ago."

"Perhaps she ran into one of her friends and has gotten caught up in conversation," Trent tried to reassure her.

"My daughter would have heard the bell and returned by now. Something is not right, my lord."

Trent steered her back to the box. The duchess relayed her findings to her husband, and as he listened, he made a decision.

"I'll go make some inquiries. Like I said earlier, Your Grace, perhaps she's simply with friends."

"Thank you, Trent," the duke replied.

"I'm sure I'll find her." He nodded to both gentlemen and turned to leave.

Trent headed down the stairs to the front door. If she'd left, someone would have had to see her. It occurred to him that Northshire had disappeared during the intermission. As much as he didn't want to go there, his thoughts ran one scenario over and over in his head. Had the old duke followed Lady Eugenie and forced her out of the theater?

His darkest fear was soon met with truth as two footmen watching the front door to the theater confirmed what had been on his mind. The Duke of Northshire had indeed kidnapped Lady Eugenie.

They relayed to him how the duke had her by the arm as he removed her from the theater and across the street to his waiting carriage. A traveling carriage. One a person would have for long hauls on the roads. Two others confirmed the doormen's story as Trent began to inquire as to which way the duke's carriage had gone.

He raced back into the theater and was met in the lobby by the Duke of Brandon and his own father. He relayed his findings, and the three decided Trent would go immediately to the mews and ride his stallion in search of Northshire. First stop would be the duke's London home, though Trent doubted the man would take Eugenie there.

Trent swung his leg over his stallion's back. He could cover a lot more distance on horseback than in a hackney. He could stop by the duke's, and knowing they wouldn't be there, he could question the butler. Once the man learned what his employer had done, chances were the man wouldn't hide the duke's whereabouts.

Would he chance taking Lady Eugenie to one of his lesser estates, or did he have something else in mind? Trent wondered if Northshire was going to try and make her agree to a marriage between them. He was that desperate and would now stop at nothing.

He reined in his stallion in the front of Northshire's London home. The house was dark except for one light in a front window and a torch that shown on the front of the house. A sleepy looking footman appeared from nowhere to take the reins of Trent's horse. He quickly found out the duke had not returned from the theater, that he'd informed the butler he was leaving for a small estate he owned outside Somerset.

Was this a ruse, and the duke was merely biding his time in order to get Lady Eugenie out of London, or was he that ignorant of the fact people would be looking for her the moment it was discovered she'd been abducted?

The coach had been seen heading north, away from the coast. Trent rode to the Duke of Brandon's home to inform Eugenie's father of what he'd discovered. They'd devise a plan and split up into smaller groups. He couldn't be too far ahead, which was exactly why he needed to get on the road as quickly as possible.

A groom met him in front of Brandon's London

home. Trent ran up the steps, and the butler led him to the duke's study, where the two men were deep in discussion.

"No luck?" Brandon asked.

"No, but I didn't think he'd be so reckless as to return home. His man said the duke mentioned going to his estate outside Somerset."

"You don't believe he went there?" his father inquired.

Trent shook his head. "No, he was seen heading north, and he was in his traveling carriage with Lady Eugenie at his side."

"We'll need more men to help us," Brandon said flatly.

"If you gentlemen will search London and the surrounding areas, I'm going to ride and see if I can catch up with the duke's carriage. If he's headed north on the road as the groom and footmen told me, he shouldn't be too far ahead."

At that moment, Viscount Radstock walked into the duke's study. "I heard what happened and thought you could use some assistance."

Trent explained everything to his friend, who nodded as he took it all in.

"I'm heading north. Care to join me? We can split up if need be once we're out of town."

"Come, we're wasting time sitting here. Northshire is only getting further away," Radstock muttered.

LADY EUGENIE SAT huddled in the corner of the Duke of Northshire's traveling coach, trying to get her wits about herself. The duke had dragged her out of the theater, pistol stuck in her side, demanding she stay quiet or else. His man had stuffed her into the carriage and now sat across from her and Northshire. The curtains were drawn, and Eugenie had lost all sense of direction. She had no idea which way they were headed. The only thing she did know was that Northshire was desperate.

She kept her eyes shut, reminding herself that her absence was probably already noticed and that Lord Trent and others would start looking for her. The marquess would also realize Northshire had disappeared right around the same time.

"Where are you taking me?" she spat as she finally opened her eyes. She'd learn nothing by feigning sleep, and it was obvious the duke and his man weren't going to talk between themselves in her presence.

"To your new home, my dear, where you'll be pampered like the duchess you were born to be," Northshire replied.

He had a smug look on his face that Eugenie wished she could slap right off. Unfortunately, that brut of a man traveling with them probably wouldn't allow it. She needed to get a sense of where they were headed, and she must act with a level head.

"I understand you have many estates, Your Grace. I was merely curious as to which one."

"Stop talking. Now! Where we are going is none of your concern," the duke snarled.

"But why did you kidnap me, Your Grace?" Eugenie persisted.

"You refused to take my advances seriously. When I went to speak with your father about my interest in wedding you, he brushed me aside. Told me you were already promised to another."

Eugenie tried to hide her shock. She needed to keep her wits in order to find a time to escape. It wouldn't be easy, but sooner or later they would have to stop to either change the team out or rest themselves. She doubted the second would happen. Wherever

Northshire was taking her, he had no intentions to make their journey comfortable.

"Arranged marriages are nothing new, Your Grace. The Duke of Marlborough's son and I have known for years what our fate would be."

"Yet, I have ruined your plans. We shall wed. It's all arranged."

"Never! I'll never marry you."

He arched a brow, the smirk of superiority returning to his face. "I suggest you cease speaking and rest. We have a long journey ahead of us. I would hate for my bride to have circles under her eyes when we wed."

"You'll never get away with this," she spat.

Northshire laughed. The carriage was dark with the exception of one lantern that shone. His features looked distorted in the dim light. "I already am, my dear. Now quiet yourself, or I'll have Todd here make your journey a bit more uncomfortable."

The large hulk of a man merely smiled at her. He'd enjoy nothing more than to gag and bind her, which was why the duke had him along. If the duke were on his own, Eugenie felt sure she could get away. He was slow in his movements. His man, on the other hand, seemed quite fit. She stood no chance of escape with him nearby.

Her body gave way to the movement of the carriage, and she fell asleep. For how long she was unsure, but she silently cursed herself for having done so. She had woken when the steady movement of the coach slowed before coming to a stop. Orders were being given, and the duke's man stepped outside to oversee whatever was going on. This left her alone with the duke.

"We're changing teams. There is some bread, cheese, and wine in a basket under the seat. I'll have Todd get it when he returns."

"I'm not hungry, Your Grace. I would, however, like to be allowed to take care of my own needs, if I may?"

"Not here. Not where someone might see you. Once we're back on the road, I'll make sure the carriage stops a safe distance from here. You may tend to your needs then."

"But. . ."

"Silence!" he barked. He sat forward and lifted the curtain ever so slightly. She was sitting across from him and in a corner. His line of sight was obscured to her.

All she knew was they were at a coaching inn of some sort. But where? And which direction were they headed? She needed to stop and think and try to remember where some of the duke's lesser estates might be. He'd never risk taking her to his main country estate. It would be the first place Trent or anyone else went to look for her.

Had she heard her father or anyone else make mention of properties Northshire owned?

The carriage slowly pulled away just as the duke's man Todd climbed in. He said something inaudible to him. Whatever it was, the duke nodded his head in agreement. Northshire said something in return to the man, and the man nodded with a smirk.

They weren't back on the road long when rain began to fall. She felt the temperature drop, but neither man offered her a blanket or any other comfort. Her gown offered little in the way of keeping her warm.

A few minutes later, the duke said something to his man, and Todd in turn smirked and tapped on the roof of the carriage. It came to a stop, the rain still beating down. The bulky man opened the door and jumped down. He lowered the steps and offered Eugenie his hand.

"You may go no further than those bushes. Do not

dally or think you can escape. I'll be watching," the man said gruffly.

Eugenie removed her hand from his meatier one and huffed off to tend to her needs. In the faint sliver of a moon, she could see nothing around her she recognized. There were three other men in addition to the driver. Escape would be impossible, especially in this light.

She took one final look around before leaving the somewhat privacy of the bushes. It was impossible to tell which direction they traveled as the moon was too high in the sky. She knew little of direction except for what Trent and her own brother had taught her. Women weren't supposed to have an interest in such things. At this very moment, she wished she'd paid better attention to what they had taught her.

Todd stood on the other side of the bushes and led her back to the carriage door. She brushed off his attempt to assist her back inside. Once they were underway, Northshire offered her a hunk of cheese and bread. He passed her a wine skin to drink from. Creature comforts were not a concern to either of them.

The bread tasted old and chewy. The cheese had no flavor, and the wine was nothing spectacular. She accepted it all, unsure if they would stop anywhere along the way for a meal. As she ate, her mind wandered to Trent. She had no doubt he'd organized search parties to look for her. She could be anywhere, but with their fathers' and his resources, she had no doubt they would leave no stone unturned.

CHAPTER 8

$\mathcal{T}$rent pushed Solomon on as the rain pelted down. He had no time to stop for the rain. Every second counted, and if Northshire was traveling in a traveling carriage, he would only stop to change teams. Depending on where they were headed. That was the question.

He'd sent Radstock along another north bound road that led to the west, while another small group headed toward Somerset. Trent knew Northshire would never go to any of his better-known estates. He would take her to one of his lesser pieces of property. One he might only visit once a year.

His father had mentioned that the duke's younger brother was a vicar and had served on the Archbishop of Canterbury's staff until a year ago. After some sort of scandal, the vicar had been reassigned to a remote village in the north. A village where Northshire had a small, little used estate. It was farmed by tenants for grain. The house was said to be in dire need of repairs and held little interest to the duke.

Trent wondered if the duke's brother kept residence at the estate or at the vicarage like most priests did. The thought of the duke having a vicar for a brother terrified him as he tried not to think of the fact that the duke could be taking Eugenie there for his brother to marry them. They'd be able to stay virtually unnoticed if the duke were smart.

Radstock was traveling to a little-known estate Northshire owned outside Liverpool. The duke had inherited the property from his mother's brother upon his death and held on to it, he'd been told, for one of his lesser children. Children born after an heir or even a daughter. But it seemed unlikely he would take Eugenie there.

Trent was sure the duke would take her to be near his brother so he could marry them. He had to stop them, stop a farce of a marriage from happening. He would make it by the following evening if he rode hard. He knew he could only push Solomon so far without rest.

His friend Heath lived a few hours off. Perhaps he could leave his stallion there to rest and borrow one of the viscount's fine horses to continue the remainder of the way. Then would come the hard part. Northshire would have men guarding his estate and Lady Eugenie. Getting anywhere near her might be more difficult than he anticipated. He would have to observe the comings and goings from afar to make his next move. He would also need a plan when he did take Eugenie. Somewhere where they didn't have to be on the road traveling too long. Northshire's men would follow. It would be too far to try making it back to Heath's estate. Inns were out of the question unless he found one far off the main road, and they were few and far between.

The rain was relentless, slowing him down more than he wished. The sky was lightening; dawn would be upon them shortly. His mind shifted to Lady Eugenie, wondering how she was faring and how well the duke was taking care of her. He knew Eugenie well enough to know she wouldn't be fearful of the duke and would be looking for ways to escape, though the rain might keep her from fleeing if she had the chance. It would be too hard for her to travel in her gown.

He had to find her and find her quickly.

A coaching inn appeared on the side of the road. He turned Solomon near. He wasn't far from Heath's, and he could at least water his stallion and let him rest for a short period of time before riding on to his friend's residence. While he was waiting, he would ask questions and see if a traveling carriage had come through. Perhaps this was where the duke might have changed teams.

He dismounted in front of the stables and left instruction for Solomon's care while he went into the tap room at the inn. The stallion seemed grateful for the break, though he would have gladly gone on without hesitation for Trent.

The tap room was sparse of customers. He ordered an ale and sat at a table nearest a window. As much as he would like to eat, he knew it would only slow him down. Still, Solomon needed a break, and a bowl of stew would fill him and warm him.

A lone serving wench, probably the proprietor's daughter, brought him a bowl of mutton stew, a hunk of bread and cheese, along with a second ale. He decided to ask the buxom blonde if anyone fitting the old duke's description might have passed through. For once, he was in luck.

There had been a fancy traveling coach with a crest on the doors that had stopped long enough to change out their team for a fresh one. The curtains had been pulled down, and she'd seen no one but a man servant who purchased two skins of ale and took care of payment with her father. No one else outside the coachmen had been seen before they left. They seemed to be in a hurry as the man refused her father when he offered a meal.

When he inquired how long ago this occurred, the young woman replied it couldn't have been more than an hour, hour and a half at best. Not too far ahead of him, especially in the wet weather. The blonde did mention her father had been concerned about the condition of the roads in the continuing rain, but the man servant and coachman were not concerned. They were far more interested in getting to whatever their destination was.

The proprietor gruffly called his daughter back to the kitchens, and she bobbed, gave him a wink, and left him to his meal and ale. Trent forced himself to finish as much of the stew as he could stomach as he pondered what to do next. What would he do if he came upon the coach? He was only one man, and Northshire had men with him. His best move would be to follow at a safe distance so as not to be seen.

Trouble was, did he dare leave and return to the spot he and Radstock had agreed to meet the following evening? He wondered if the destination Northshire was going was only a stopping point, a place to rest before moving on.

Well one thing was for sure; he had to have some help.

LADY EUGENIE TRIED to feign she was sleeping. Anything to keep her from having to speak with either of the despicable men sharing the carriage with her. It hardly mattered one way or another if they believed she was asleep or not.

Judging time, especially since the coach had stopped and switched out teams, was nearly impossible. With the curtains still drawn, Eugenie had no concept of where they might be, no sense of direction, or even what time of night it might be.

Her thoughts drifted to her father and mother, something she'd tried avoiding all night. If she allowed herself to become too emotional, she would forget what her ultimate goal was. The duchess was not one who could handle anything that was not in her perfectly ordered life. Eugenie figured her mother would have done one of two things by now. She would have either taken to her bed, too distraught to be comforted, or she would bathe in the attention the wives of other peers assisting her father in finding her lavished her with.

The duke, on the other hand, would be frantic to find her. He might have planned her future himself with his matchmaking, but she knew he would never tolerate anyone kidnapping her. Not even a peer such as the Duke of Northshire. No doubt he'd have all of England looking for her, and would most likely have had Lord Trent's father, the Duke of Marlborough, send word to his Scottish son-in-law and daughter to watch for them at the border. Northshire was desperate, and Gretna Green couldn't be ruled out.

The rain was still pelting down against the carriage as it had been for hours. The condition of the roads must be deteriorating because Eugenie could sense the team had slowed. The coachman would have to be careful in order to avoid the team or carriage from slipping.

She felt the carriage slow even more, the horses brought to a brisk walk as they turned a corner. Where were they going? She didn't have to ponder much longer. The coach came to a stop. The henchman traveling inside with her and Northshire had been anything but quiet as he opened the door and jumped down into what sounded like mud and rain.

"Come," Northshire said impatiently, grabbing her arm. "The roads are getting too treacherous to travel. We'll stay here until the rain ends."

Eugenie descended the carriage and quickly glanced around at her surroundings. Dawn was indeed upon them, and in spite of the rain, she could clearly make out a large structure with a thatched roof. They were in the middle of a forest, she assumed, judging by all the trees surrounding them.

Northshire dragged her across a mud filled clearing to the cottage. Inside, a coachman was busy building a fire, another lighting lamps. She quickly deduced this was a hunting lodge, obviously owned by the duke as he was far too familiar with it as he strode about.

Their eyes locked, and the older man grinned, knowing he had the upper hand. "Did you really think I would take you to one of my estates? I'm hardly that stupid. Your father has sent search parties out I'm sure, so we'll stay here."

"For how long, my lord?"

He snorted. "Until the rain stops. It's getting far too dangerous to travel at such a speed. The men are tired and wet, and the horses need a good rest. No one will think to look here."

"Why would no one look here, my lord?"

"Because few know of its existence."

She tried not to let her emotions cloud her. He didn't need to know she was disappointed but not surprised.

"You seem to have thought of everything," she whispered.

Ignoring her bitter comment, he led her to a door leading into a bedchamber. Another fireplace was being tended to by another of his henchmen, and though there were no windows in the room, it was appealing and comfortable looking.

"You'll stay here. A man will stand guard outside the door," he said gruffly. "In case you have any ideas of escaping. Do as you're told, and your life will be so much easier. Test me, and you'll find an entirely different side of me."

The fire blazing, the young man left the room, leaving her completely alone as the door shut behind the duke and him. Looking around, Eugenie found a narrow bed against one wall. There were more than enough blankets stacked at the foot. A nearby chair placed in front of the fire was the only other piece of furniture outside a massive wardrobe placed on another wall.

She opted to sit in front of the fire and grabbed a blanket from the bed before sitting down. Eugenie found herself exhausted. She knew she needed to stay awake, but her body wasn't going to allow it. She needed to rest and maintain her strength in case she got a chance to escape.

It didn't take her long to fall asleep, waking only to the sound of thunder rumbling overhead. The rain was beating down on the thatched roof. The room was cool, the fire needing to be restored. Rising from the uncomfortable wood chair, she picked up a couple of scraps of wood and threw them into the embers.

As she waited for the fire, she pulled the blanket around her and walked toward the door. She heard nothing, no muffled voice or anything else. She wondered if this meant everyone was asleep. If she opened the door, would she be forced back inside by one of the men the duke had guarding her, or could he possibly be asleep?

She could use one of several excuses she'd thought up. It would give her a reason for being out of the room if questioned, which she undoubtedly would be. There was no more wood to add to the fire; that would be perfect, along with there was nothing to poke the logs around with.

After that, food and tending to her personal needs were on her list. She paused at the closed door and inhaled. Her hand on the handle, she pulled it toward her. It opened without a problem, and before she could step out of the room, she was met by a lanky, young coachman she remembered from earlier.

"I'm sorry, my lady, but I cannot let you pass. Tell me what you require, and I'll see to it."

She retreated back into the room, sizing him up as she did. "I need more wood, something to stoke the fire, I need to tend to my own needs, and lastly, I am quite hungry."

"Let me see what I can do, my lady," he replied as he began to shut the door, adding, "If you look behind the screen in the far corner, I'm sure you'll find what you need. I'll see to the rest."

Disappointed, Eugenie retreated back into the room. She hadn't really taken the time to look around since there were no windows. She'd failed to see the screen. Walking over to it, she found a small table with a basin and pitcher with water and underneath a simple chamber pot. Ugh, with all the new innovations, this was one from the past she could live without, but she reminded herself it was better than being out in the woods.

She tended to herself before returning to the fire. As she did, she noted the hem of her dress was damp and muddy, her slippers ruined. Truly, ladies' footwear was not meant for walking in the forest or anywhere else.

Her boots would have been the only thing keeping her from being barefoot. She placed her slippers on the hearth in front of her and hoped for the best.

A few minutes later the door opened, and the young man guarding her entered with another. He carried a stack of firewood while her guard placed a tray containing what she assumed was her breakfast. A pot of tea along with a loaf of bread and some cheese. She wondered where it had come from and was curious if the duke hadn't planned this as well.

Before leaving, the one carrying the firewood stoked the fire and added more wood. Another jolt of thunder cracked above them.

"Where is the duke? I should like to speak with him," she said as the young men began to leave.

"His Grace is still abed, my lady. I'm sure he'll come see you when he wakes."

She nodded. She really wasn't thrilled about having to speak with the duke. After all, he had grand ideas for what he had envisioned for the two of them. How would he accomplish this with everyone on the lookout for them? At least she hoped someone was out scanning the countryside looking for her. Trent would never let her down.

Not having any real sense of where they were, she couldn't judge what Northshire might have in mind for her. In truth, she knew very little about the duke, except for the fact that he was a notorious braggart, a gambler, and thought himself far more important than he actually was. He was a duke, but aside from that, she knew he felt the need to portray himself in a different light. A more successful one.

What could her father have been thinking to even speak with this horrid man?

It dawned on her, perhaps he'd done so to encourage Trent into making a marriage offer. They both knew their fathers wished them to marry, and both had hesitated. What if her father, in all his wisdom, used Northshire as a means to get Trent to offer for her?

It was well within the scope of possibilities. Trent thought there was another reason, one they hadn't found. If he'd figured it out, he hadn't shared it with her yet.

Why did life have to be so complicated? As if hers wasn't already, Northshire had decided to add to it. She had to figure out how to get away from the duke and his henchmen.

Eugenie was sitting by the fire, listening to the rain falling on the roof, trying to stay warm when Northshire finally made his first appearance. He was as smug and self-righteous as he'd been when he'd abducted her.

"Good morning, my love," he purred. He neared her, running his fingers through her hair, which now hung free below her shoulders. Without a mirror, there had been little she could do besides attempt to pin it up.

"Quit calling me that. I'm not your love," she hissed.

"Oh, but you are. It's best you stop fighting me and learn to accept the way your life is set to be."

"Never!"

He motioned to the young footman who'd brought her the tray earlier. "He's going to see to whatever it is you need. Within reason, of course." The young man went behind the screen and fetched the chamber pot and quietly left the room.

"Where are we?" Eugenie asked.

The duke brushed her off. "Nowhere you need to concern yourself with. Unfortunately, the rain has slowed us down, so until it stops, we're forced to stay here."

Eugenie's brow knit together angrily. "I believe I

have every right to know where I am. You, Your Grace, abducted me and have yet to give me a reason as to why or where it is you're taking me."

"My dearest Eugenie, I didn't abduct you. I merely persuaded you to join me on our wedding trip."

"Wedding trip?"

"Yes, we're to be married as soon as we reach our destination."

"Gretna Green? Is that where you're taking me?" she asked. "I can assure you my father and the Duke of Marlborough will have sent riders there in search of me."

He laughed. It was disgusting to her ears. "Gretna Green? Heavens no. They'll be chasing their own tails going there. No, I have something else planned for our wedding."

"There will be no wedding between us, Your Grace."

His face darkened as he got as close as possible. "You are mine, understood? You need to get it out of your head that anyone is going to rescue you. No one knows where you are and will not until I choose to reveal your whereabouts. By then we'll be married, and hopefully, you'll carry my child."

"So, I'm your prisoner?"

His lip curled up before answering. "Your words, not mine, my love."

"I can assure you I will fight you every inch of the way, and if should I be forced to wed you, my father or Marlborough will see to it such a union is annulled, and you, sir, will be a person non gratis in society," she spat. She walked away from him.

"Obviously, you need some time to get used to the idea, my dear. I'm going to leave you to reflect on what we've discussed. Hopefully, you'll see things my way."

Eugenie heard the door latch shut and knew the duke had left her. She had to figure out a way to escape.

The rain would surely slow her down. If she could just see outside for herself, get some bearing as to her surroundings.

In the meantime, she'd simply have to pray that her father's men or Trent would find her soon.

CHAPTER 9

rent had brought Solomon to a walk. The mixture between wet and slick roads and the rain had slowed him down immensely. The rain had not stopped, thus making traveling virtually impossible, if not dangerous. He would not allow harm to come to his stallion because of his own stupidity.

There was a lone rider in front of him, coming off a fork in the road ahead. He immediately recognized the rider as Radstock. He, too, looked soaked, cold, and miserable.

"I'm surprised to see you," he told Radstock.

"Likewise. I found no one matching Northshire's description, so I turned and hoped I'd meet up with you."

"They were only about an hour or hour and a half ahead of me. I stopped at a coaching inn to let Solomon rest and to eat, and was told a fancy traveling coach with a crest on the doors had pulled out about an hour before me."

"You should have been able to catch up with the coach; the rain would have slowed them down."

Trent nodded. "Agreed. So where are they?"

"We're miles from a city and even miles to the next village, if my mind remembers correctly."

"You're correct; there's nothing but farm land and some good-sized forests between here and the next village."

Radstock shifted in his saddle. "No one will be on the road today. There is another coaching inn about two miles ahead. Why don't we stop there, let the horses rest, and dry off and have a hot meal?"

Trent hesitated.

"You'll do Lady Eugenie no good if you're cold, hungry, tired, and wet. Perhaps this inn may have seen them," Radstock muttered. "Besides, they'd have to go right past the inn if they traveled this way."

Trent began walking. "Come, perhaps we can learn more from someone at the inn. A carriage such as the duke's is sure to have drawn attention."

"You're right. At least we should be able to get a better sense as to where we are."

Trent walked alongside his friend until he could stand being slow no more. He urged the stallion into a trot. Two miles would seem like forever if ridden at a walk in this rain. The sooner he found the duke and his party, the sooner he could return Eugenie to her father.

When he did, he would formally ask for her. If there was one thing he'd learned riding all this way it was that his feelings for Lady Eugenie were far greater than simple childhood friendship and feelings. For that, he'd let no other man court or marry her.

No one at the coaching inn could remember a coach matching Northshire's having stopped either to change out teams or take a meal. None had been seen going by, either. The tap room was busy with travelers who were doing as they were, getting out of the weather.

Radstock ordered them both an ale and dinner. The inn owner offered a private dining room, which they accepted. It was quiet, the food a step up from the tap room, and it gave them a chance to go over where they'd both been and where they should head next.

"If no one saw the coach, and they didn't pass you, and they didn't take the road where I came from—where are they?" Radstock asked.

"We've missed something."

Radstock took a long sip of ale as he mulled over what they knew. "There must be an estate or a private road somewhere between the two inns."

"Perhaps we should ask someone," Trent said as the serving girl brought two plates with roast chicken, vegetables, and bread.

"Are there any private estates, roads leading to them around here?" Radstock asked her as she set the plate in front of him.

"No, my lord. There are some private hunting lodges, but I'm not sure where."

"Who owns these private lodges?" Trent asked.

"Not sure. Not even sure where they are."

"Is there anyone else we could ask?"

The girl smiled. "I can ask around, my lord."

"Please do. It's important."

The serving girl nodded and quit the room, leaving Trent and Radstock alone with their dinner.

"Hunting lodges. I would almost agree, except I never saw any sort of roads leading to one."

"Unless it's rarely used."

"Even so," Radstock said, "there should be some indication."

"We'll ask the proprietor; he would know. Or he'd know someone who might know. It would have to be somewhere far enough off the main road to be able to hide that flashy coach."

"Do you really think he'll force Lady Eugenie into marriage?"

"Yes, he's desperate for funds, and her dowry is very attractive to any man."

Radstock sat back in his chair and took a long drink of ale. "You really care for her, don't you?"

Trent nodded. "I believe I've fallen in love with her."

"Don't worry; we'll find her. I have faith in our abilities."

"The first thing we must do is inquire with the proprietor about hunting lodges, because if Northshire owns one near here, the man would have to know."

Radstock pushed back his chair from the table and rose to his full height. "Let me get us another ale. I'll see the proprietor comes and joins us."

"Excellent idea."

Trent sat contemplating their next move while his friend went in search of more ale and the owner of the establishment. It was obvious they'd be here a while; between the horses needing to rest and the miserable weather, there was little more they could do but sit and wait.

It wasn't uncommon for aristocrats to own property separate from their estates where they could go with friends to hunt and be men. The hunting lodges were usually built in the middle of a forest, out of sight to others.

He thought about what he'd just told Radstock. Yes, he'd always been quite fond of Lady Eugenie, but over time, he'd noticed his feelings for her changing into something deeper. Learning Northshire had absconded with her from beneath not only his, but her own father's nose had unnerved him. Finding her had become his sole purpose. He would not see her harmed by anyone, and the thought of Northshire forcing her into marriage made his blood boil.

He finished off his ale just as Radstock and the inn's owner came through the door. The man placed another tankard of ale in front of him before sitting down at their table. Radstock shut the door.

"Your friend said you had some questions?" the man inquired. He was an older man; he was well-known around these parts as having one of the nicer establishments. Aristocrats would ride out of their way to stay here rather than some rat infested hell hole.

"Hunting lodges? Do you know of any nearby?" Trent asked the man. His gaze never moved from the man's face even as he took a sip of ale.

The man shook his head. "I can't say I do."

"What about estates? Who lives around here?" Trent pushed the man.

"We're on the backside of the Viscount Samuel's estate. We rarely see the viscount except when he makes his semi-annual trip here. His estate here is a secondary as he prefers another in Kent, I believe," the man offered.

"But no one, as far as you know, owns a hunting lodge? Or might the viscount own one he lets to friends and colleagues?" Radstock asked as he sat down next to Trent.

"Like I said, I know of no one having hunting lodges in these parts."

Trent took a sip of ale and eyed the man. "I thank you for your information, sir."

"Happy to help, my lord."

"I hope you won't mind, but we'll be staying a while. Our horses are spent, and we both are tired from our travels," Trent continued.

"I'm afraid I can't offer you a room, my lord. As you can imagine, the bad weather is good for my business. You're welcome to stay of course."

Radstock offered the man a small pouch of coins. "If you don't mind, we'll stay in here for now."

"Of course. Just let my daughter know should you require anything at all."

"We will, and thank you for your information and hospitality," Trent replied.

Trent picked up his tankard and drank before setting it down. "Do you think he was being truthful?"

"About not knowing if there were hunting lodges? Yes. What would he have to gain by lying?"

"I don't know. The one thing I do know is Northshire's carriage has disappeared."

Radstock grabbed a piece of cheese from the plate in front of them. "You know, it is possible Northshire had this better thought out than we're giving him credit for. What if he had another carriage, a less noticeable one waiting, say on a secondary road?"

"But we haven't seen one."

"Perhaps. Would we pay attention to a carriage with no markings? One that isn't as noticeable as the one he left town in?"

Trent shook his head. "No, we probably wouldn't give one a second thought. We've been going about this all wrong. We've assumed he's still in his traveling carriage."

"Which means he could be anywhere with Lady Eugenie."

"What do we actually know about the man?"

Radstock cocked his head. "What do you mean?"

"Where are his estates, land, where does his family reside?"

"Ah, does he have any brothers or sisters?"

Trent nodded. "Yes, what do we really know about him?"

Taking a bite of cheese, Radstock stared at the fire. "I recall he had a younger brother. As a second or third son, he was sent off to join the church. Last I think I heard, he was living in India teaching Christianity."

"India is too far away. Who else might he go to?"

"He'd never take Lady Eugenie to anyone other than a trusted family member, but outside of his brother, I know of none."

"So what do we do now?" Trent asked his friend. "Do we continue north to Gretna Green on the chance he takes her there, or do we return to London?"

"I think we ride on to the next village and ask questions. Someone has to have seen something no matter how small."

"You're right. If he is in the area, he'll need supplies. If he's not, someone's had to have seen his fancy carriage. Northshire's not that smart a man."

"Excellent, then we're in agreement. We'll ride to the next, closest village and ask around."

"I'll send word to my father and Lady Eugenie's from there. Let them know where we are and our findings."

This was the best they had to work with at the moment. Sooner or later they would find something or someone who'd seen them or had heard something.

EUGENIE KNEW she had to keep her wits about her. She watched as the young footman placed a tray on a small table near the fire. She needed to befriend the young man; she needed someone who would either help her escape or would at least tell her information, no matter how insignificant.

"What's your name?" she asked as she neared the tray and young man.

"His Grace says I'm not to talk with you, my lady."

"Does he now? I don't see how telling me your name

would be of any harm. If you're going to be looking after my needs, I should like to at least know your name. You know, to properly thank you."

He looked at her with a hard, cold stare. "His Grace said you'd try to trick me. It won't work."

Eugenie turned away and sat back down in the chair near the hearth. "Fine, don't tell me. I don't want to know your name. I'm not trying to trick you. I was merely being polite." She swept her hand out for dramatic effect as though dismissing him.

"I didn't mean to offend you, my lady," he said softly.

"No harm done," she replied, 'but you do know who my father is and what the duke is doing by abducting me."

"'Tis not my place to say anything, my lady." He paused and edged toward the door. "I'll check back on you later. If you need anything, knock on the door."

He was gone, and once again Eugenie was alone. She didn't mind though. Anything that kept Northshire out of sight. She had at least planted a seed in the young man's head. She had said the word—abducted. With any luck, the young man would now begin to question his loyalties to such a man.

With no window, she had no concept of time unless someone came in the room or she heard something on the other side of the door. Right now, it seemed quiet.

The way everything had fallen into place made her wonder how well organized her abduction was. The duke had not randomly chosen the theater to take her. He knew she would be there and that at some point, being a lady, she would need to make use of a retiring room. He'd used the bad weather to his advantage. What she couldn't explain was if the cottage was part of his plans or if the weather had forced them off the road. It had to belong to the duke because he was far too familiar with the structure and land around it.

Therefore, she surmised she must be on one of his estates. But which? And how long would they remain here? She was sure Northshire had something else in mind. He'd said as much. He intended to marry her, which meant he needed funds. Every man in the aristocracy knew her dowry was one of the most generous.

If they stayed here for a day or two, they would be off to wherever it was he intended to marry her. It could even be here, though Eugenie doubted it. No, he would want to marry her somewhere more comfortable. He would want to show off whatever wealth he did have in an effort to impress her.

The duke was determined to marry her. Would he take her to Gretna Green and risk the possibility of his attempt being thwarted by her father, Trent's father, or even Trent himself? The most logical answer was he would take her to one of his lesser estates and would have some cleric he'd bribed marry them. There was nothing this man wouldn't do to get more money.

The idea repulsed her. Just thinking of his clammy hands touching her repulsed her. The further idea of him being intimate with her made her want to vomit. There was no way she'd allow this to happen. She would fight him tooth and nail.

She would continue to try and make a friend in the young man who brought her meals and saw to her needs. She believed once he had a chance to think things through, he would change his mind. At least if he could do something as simple as warn her of what was to come, it would help her make decisions.

Her thoughts turned to her parents. Her mother had to be frantic by now, as well as her father. The duke would be angry, as would Trent's father. They'd made this arrangement of their two children, and now it was in jeopardy.

She also knew her father had vast connections and

would have any marriage Northshire might force on her annulled as soon as she was found. But would that be enough? What man would have her if she were ruined by the duke?

Trent would.

Once she was found, she made a vow she would accept her fate. She would marry Trent. He would be a loving and understanding husband. He knew her far better than most and would grant her the freedom to pursue her dreams.

She wondered where he was. She imagined him on that huge black stallion scorching the earth, looking everywhere for her. She knew deep in her heart Trent would not rest until she was found, and she prayed that would be soon.

For now, she would bide her time, act submissive, but observe, always keeping her ears and eyes open to what was going on around her.

The rain, though not as bad as it had been, had left a chill and dampness hanging in the air. She rose and added a couple of logs to the fire. Looking down at herself, she was horrified to see her gown anything but pressed and fresh. Anyone could see she'd not changed in quite some time, which could be to her advantage should they have to travel more to get to wherever the duke was taking her.

Eugenie couldn't remember the last time she'd slept, and sitting in front of the warmth of the fire made her relax. She closed her eyes briefly. Did she dare nap? Certainly, a couple of minutes would refresh her and she needed her mind to be sharp and clear. She shut her eyes.

When she woke up, it was to the sound of the young man the duke had placed in charge of her. He was attempting to get her attention without startling her.

"My lady. . .my lady."

"Yes? Are we leaving?"

"No, but His Grace wants you to dine with him."

"When? Now?"

"Yes, my lady."

Well, if he didn't care what her appearance was, she wasn't going to bother making an attempt. Perhaps he would see what he'd done, abducting her without much thought to her needs. She certainly didn't have another dress she could change into. She would make do with what she had.

She rose from the chair and followed the young man. She caught a horrified look on his face. Most likely because of her manner of dress and unkempt appearance.

"Don't worry, boy. I have been given no comforts. His Grace will simply have to deal with it. If he wants perfection, he'll allow me a bath and will furnish some appropriate clothing."

The young man simply nodded, not sure how he should answer. He simply led her to the main room of the cottage where the duke was seated at a dining table. The duke took one look at her appearance, and horror crossed his face.

"My dear, please bear with me. Your creature comforts will be seen to as soon as we reach our final destination."

Eugenie sat down. "And where is our final destination, Your Grace?"

"You needn't concern yourself with such matters. Final preparations are being made for our arrival. A dressmaker will be sent for so you might have a new wardrobe sewn. You'll of course want a wedding gown constructed," he said with a smirk.

"And I've told you, Your Grace, that it'll be a cold day in hell when I marry you."

"Still as wild as ever I see." He brushed a hand dramatically in the air. "It matters not. Your attitude will change soon."

Eugenie picked up a fork and picked at the roast chicken before her. She wondered how the duke had had such a meal prepared. He and his lackeys weren't able to cook, and if they did, it would be the most basic.

"Do you intend to keep me in the windowless room, Your Grace?"

His answer came without hesitation. "Indeed, I'll keep you in there as long as possible. Until we proceed on our journey."

She took a bite of chicken. It was rather savory, and she hadn't realized how hungry she really was until now. "When might that be?"

He laughed, picked up a piece of bread, and soaked it in the juice from the chicken. "So curious, but you mustn't worry your pretty head about details."

"I merely ask because I was curious how long you intend to keep me so neglected, Your Grace."

"It would do you good to learn a wife is seen, not heard."

"But I'm not your wife, nor will I ever be. Your Grace." She smiled and speared another piece of chicken. She cut up the potatoes with her fork after and savored the flavor of roasted potatoes.

"The weather clears, and we'll proceed in due time, my dear." He pointed at her plate with his knife. "Now finished your dinner."

She dropped her fork in the middle of the plate. "I believe I've had enough, Your Grace. I find the current company and conversation has ruined my appetite." She rose to her full height. "If you'll excuse me."

She rose to leave and headed back to the window-less room. She would not let him think he was winning because he controlled her every move. He didn't, and she needed desperately to find a way to escape.

Behind her she could hear the duke fuming and sputtering at what he would consider a lack of respect and manners on her part. The hell with him. The sooner he learned she was not one to be pushed and ordered around, the better.

Eugenie walked down the short hall to the closed door. She opened it, walked through, and slammed it shut right in the young footman's face. They needed to know just how displeased she was. Somehow she had to get this young man on her side. She had to figure out where she was and get away from the duke. She needed someone to help her; escaping would be near impossible without some assistance. Right now, any sense of direction she might have had was gone. Arriving in a carriage at night with the curtains pulled had given her no sense of direction, and placed in a windowless room had not helped her at all.

Without knowing whether it was day or night, she could not plot her escape at all. She paced the floor of the small room, trying to make sense of it all, and trying to figure out how she could get away from here. She had noted it was night once again. An entire day had passed. From what little she'd seen out the one window, she was in the middle of somewhere heavily wooded. A forest, perhaps, which would mean this was most likely the duke's hunting lodge or that of a close friend. But where? Her sense of direction was completely thrown off.

She needed to keep her wits about her and not get into any more altercations with the duke. That would be her best bet. If she could stay on his good side, let him think she was resigned to whatever fate he'd chosen for her, the easier it might be to escape from him. If they stayed here, perhaps he would begin to allow her some basic freedom, such as going outdoors for a walk, or let her into the main room of the cottage.

CHAPTER 10

"My lady, my lady," Eugenie heard someone say from within the darkness of her prison. It was the young footman. He carried a candle as he quietly shut the door behind himself. Under ordinary circumstances, Eugenie might have feared for herself, but not this night.

Instead, she nodded her head. "What is it?"

"Everyone is asleep. I'm the only one awake, because it was my turn to guard the cottage."

"And the duke? Is he asleep as well?"

"He overindulged, my lady. We took him to his bed."

"He passed out? Is that what you're telling me?"

"Yes. Come quickly, we haven't a moment to lose."

He was going to help her get away. She put the ruined slippers on her feet, saying nothing. He opened the door and quietly peered around the rest of the cottage. He motioned for her to follow him. Together they made their way to the door of the cottage without a single word. Fortunately, the door was quiet as he opened it, and they both slipped out.

The moon was out this night, lighting even the thick forest. He led her to where two horses stood saddled and waiting. Eugenie stared for a moment.

"I cannot ask you to accompany me," she said,

"You cannot go out on these roads by yourself, my lady. It just isn't safe. If I stay, there's no telling how the duke shall take the fact you escaped on my watch."

"True. Come, let us lead the horses and be on our way. We need to get a good distance away from this place."

"Not to worry, my lady. The duke will be down two horses and one man. He's going to be slowed down."

She nodded and took the reins to her horse and followed the young man through the woods until they finally came upon the road. Eugenie gazed around at her surroundings. "Do you remember the way?"

"Yes, my lady. We're in the north, near York. We need to hurry and make use of the moon to get as far away from here as we can."

"Thank you," Eugenie replied. "What is your name? I don't think you've ever said."

"Because the duke told me not to. My name is Thomas, my lady. Thomas MacRae."

Eugenie knew what a risk the young man was taking by helping her escape. Northshire would make every attempt to ruin his life, so he'd never find suitable employment again in an aristocrat's staff. She would speak with her father or Trent. She was sure one of them would hire him considering the circumstances.

They spent the next hour riding hard and fast in an attempt to get as far away as they could from the duke. The full moon lit up the road like daylight. They passed a coaching inn and continued south toward London. After riding three hours Thomas suggested they find a place off the road and in the trees to rest the horses and themselves.

"We should rest for a couple of hours," Thomas said looking up at the sky as they walked along the road, trying to give the horses a break.

"I agree. We need to let the horses rest as I do not have money to change them out," Eugenie replied.

"I have some money. Probably enough to change out horses or at least feed and rest them and buy a meal."

"First, let's get off the road and rest. I'm not sure how safe these roads are this late at night."

"You're right of course." She glanced about her and pointed to a thick grove of trees. "That would suit nicely. The trees are close together, the underbrush thick, and hopefully, there is water nearby for the horses."

Together they unsaddled the horses. As Thomas led them to a nearby tree, Eugenie looked for a place for them to rest. She spread out one of the blankets from the horses next to a tree. They were far enough off the road, no one would be the wiser, but close enough they could see anyone who passed.

Thomas approached carrying a wine skin and the saddle bags he'd had behind him. He passed her the wine, and after she sat on the ground, he sat nearby and produced a hunk of cheese and a loaf of bread.

"We won't go hungry," she whispered as she took the food he offered. "We shall be fine, thanks to your quick thinking."

"At least for now," he agreed. "When dawn is upon us, I'll walk and see if I can find a stream. We can water the horses and allow them to graze even if it's for a short time."

She nodded, and they ate in silence. Eugenie hadn't realized how hungry she really was. Though she'd dined with the duke, she had eaten little before storming back into the small, windowless room. Now she was tired. She accepted a coat Thomas had brought with him and covered herself with it. He leaned up against a tree to try and sleep, while she lay down, hoping they both could rest.

Tomorrow they would ride all day. She needed to ask Thomas how many days it would take them before they returned to London. She had no sense of time, having been kept away from windows. She was grateful just to be outdoors once again.

She found herself nodding off to sleep and did nothing to prevent it. Even a couple of hours would be welcome, but they had to stay sharp. There was always the chance of highwaymen. Because of the late hour, she knew there were most likely no other riders nearby. Most would have stopped somewhere for the night or even for a few hours. She wondered how many did as they were. The last thing she could recall thinking was how much further they had yet to travel.

Eugenie awoke several hours later. Dawn was upon them. Neither Thomas nor the horses were anywhere to be found, but she quickly remembered him mentioning going to look for a place to water the horses nearby.

She didn't have to wait long. As she gathered up everything, she looked up at the sound of something moving nearby. It turned out to be Thomas leading the two horses.

"I found a stream not far from here if you wish to freshen up, my lady. I watered the horses and let them graze on some grass nearby."

"I would. Keep watch. I shall return in a few minutes."

He pointed her in the direction of the stream and walked away. She would hurry. They needed to get back on the road before a lot of other riders did. They had no idea where Northshire might be, making it pertinent that they put as much distance between them as possible.

The cool water felt good as she splashed it onto her face, and as she walked back to join Thomas, she ran her fingers through her hair. She pulled it back and tried to secure it as best she could. She must look a fright to anyone they might come upon in her mud-stained gown and ruined slippers. How many days had passed now since she was first abducted?

Thomas passed her a hunk of cheese and bread after she mounted. They walked down the road in silence, eating and keeping a close eye on everything around them. He finally passed her the wine skin, and she gratefully took a swallow.

"Do you have any idea where we are?"

"We're heading south, my lady. It was raining the night we came this way, so it was hard to pick out landmarks."

"I see. Don't you think the duke's men will know this is the way we're headed?"

"They might, but there was a road that forked off from this one."

"Perhaps we should take that road. Maybe we'll come to a village or town."

"We might, but I believe that's what the duke's men would think. No, I say we continue down this road. Eventually something will have to look familiar."

She looked up at the overcast sky. "If we don't run into rain today."

"Rain would be to our advantage, my lady."

"How's that? We can't continue on in the rain. We'll both take ill."

"It'll slow everything down, but if it rains, it won't be for quite a while," he replied, pointing to a sliver of sunlight peering through the clouds.

"Then we need to make good time before the rain sets in."

They finished their meager breakfast and pushed the horses into a slow gallop down the road.

ADMITTING defeat wasn't in Trent's vocabulary, but he and Radstock had come to the conclusion that they had no idea where to turn. No one had seen a traveling coach with ducal seals on the road since the rain stopped. They'd searched in vain for signs of a hunting lodge—a path or little used road that would lead them to such a place. Nothing.

Trent had decided that Northshire wouldn't risk taking Eugenie to Gretna Green. It would be far too risky for him. Too much road between here and the Scottish border; anything could happen. He wasn't a stupid man. He'd know Eugenie's father and he would have men scattered between London and Scotland.

It was time to return to London in case there was word. They'd done their best with no luck, though he and Radstock were still convinced the proprietor of the inn where they'd spent a rainy night knew more than he'd let on.

"I think it might be beneficial if we swung back to the coaching inn and observed the comings and goings from the woods," he told Radstock as they were walking their horses down a deserted road.

"You still think the innkeeper knows more than he's letting on?"

"I do," he replied.

Radstock sighed. "There're only two of us. What I think we need to do is continue on to London."

"Or find a town and send a telegram to my father. Let him know where we are."

"You're right. We're not too far from Leicester. I'm sure they'd have a telegraph office."

"Then let's go to Leicester," Trent replied. "By the way, how do you know we're near Leicester?"

"I have a widowed aunt who lives there. I'm sure we could stay with her if we need to."

"I don't think I've ever heard you mention her before."

"Probably because I rarely see her. Her son, the Duke of Leicester is a rake and bleeds the estate."

"How does that concern you?"

"Because my father was appointed by his brother, the late duke, to oversee the ducal estates and monies."

"I see. I would keep a distance as well. In that case, perhaps it's best we don't visit your aunt. It might be best if we stayed in town in case we get a quick response from my father."

They continued down the deserted road. Finally, Trent urged Solomon into a gallop. The stallion was restless, and Trent knew it was from being held back. Radstock followed though at a distance before they slowed back to a walk.

Trent spoke of something he'd been carrying since they'd left London. "Do you think Northshire will harm Eugenie?"

"What? Why would you ask such a thing?" Radstock shook his head. "No, I'm sure she's well looked after. He needs her far too much to harm her."

"I don't know the duke that well, other than his unnatural fondness toward Lady Eugenie."

"Yes, and we've already established it's her dowry he's after. The man's desperate for money. I would quit your worrying. I imagine Lady Eugenie can take care of herself."

Trent smiled. "Yes, Lady Eugenie is more than able to take care of herself, even with the likes of a man like the duke. She'll fight him at every turn."

"Then don't worry," Radstock replied.

Trent smiled. "But I do pity Northshire."

They laughed at the thought of the sputtering, ill-mannered Northshire being bested by a lady. After hours in the saddle, they noted more farms, more civilization all around them. Leicester wasn't far. At the top of a hill, Radstock pointed out the spire of the cathedral jutting up above the town.

"Do you know where your aunt lives?"

"Of course I do. She still lives with her son on the family estate, which is right outside town."

"First things first. Find the telegraph office and send word to my father. After that, I suggest we find a room, bathe, and change."

"Agreed. If we were to visit my aunt, Auntie Florence would probably have a case of the vapors if she saw me like this," Radstock replied, looking down at himself. It was obvious they'd been on the road for some time. Neither of them had shaved, bathed, or changed clothes in days. A tub of hot water would be a most welcome sight.

"And your cousin would most likely look down his nose at us."

"No doubt there. Matt's always been a bit of a snob. Don't know why he doesn't spend more time in London. He'd fit right in with the other rakes and dandies."

They walked their horses a while longer before Trent got irritated and finally stopped and asked about a telegraph office. The gentleman, old enough to be their father, was quick to point them in the right direction to both a hotel and the telegraph office. They were almost next door to the other, he made a point in saying.

They reined their horses in front of the hotel. Radstock swung down. "Come, let's at least procure a room, then you can send word to your father."

"Very well."

The hotel was smaller than ones found in London, but the pair were able to rent a small suite. Trent paid for two nights, in case Radstock's aunt wasn't as welcoming as he thought. They inquired about stabling the horses, and the clerk summoned a young groom to take the them.

"Be sure they are rubbed down properly and fed well. An extra ration of oats for each," Trent told the lad.

"Yes, my lord. The mews is right behind the hotel. You can't miss it. I'll get them rubbed down and stalled in no time."

"Very good. We'll check in on them later," Trent replied.

"You coddle that stallion far too much," Radstock quipped.

"He's full of energy and becomes sullen if not handled properly."

"Yes, which is why I prefer my meek gelding." Radstock laughed. "Go take care of getting word to your father. I'll go up to our suite and see that what bags we did bring are delivered. I plan on having a glass of whiskey and soaking in a tub of hot water."

The telegraph office wasn't that hard to find. Two doors down from the hotel, just like the man had told him. He quickly scratched out what he wanted delivered to his father and paid the clerk, telling him he would be staying at the hotel should his father respond quickly.

Trent found Radstock in a tub of hot water, just like he'd said he would, with a cheroot in one hand and a glass of whiskey in the other. "I hope it's okay, but I sent our clothes to be pressed."

"Fine with me. I have no plans. We'll send these down for cleaning later. At least we'll be presentable."

"I figured you'd want to hang out around here and see if your father replies quickly. We can enjoy dinner in the dining room or have it brought to us. I'm up to either."

Trent took off his great coat and jacket and hung them over the back of a chair. He loosened his cravat before walking over and pouring himself a whiskey. He then sat down in an overstuffed chair and sighed.

"It feels good to sit in a chair," he called out to Radstock.

"A bath is better," came the reply.

He didn't say a thing; he simply enjoyed the fine whiskey.

"Don't feel guilty that we aren't out looking for Eugenie," Radstock said.

"I am, but we needed to regroup. We won't be of any use to her if we're exhausted and hungry," Trent murmured. "Maybe we'll get lucky, and my father will tell me Northshire felt guilty and brought her back."

"At least they'll know where we are," Radstock replied.

"That's true. I'm hoping my father might have found out where all Northshire's properties are."

"And perhaps we're not too far away."

Not long after, Trent found himself soaking in a tub of hot water. Modern indoor plumbing was so convenient. Gone, at least in most cases, were the need for watermen to carry water upstairs. These days, water came from taps, the water heated elsewhere in the building, and the dirty water went down to the sewer. So efficient.

His thoughts trailed to Eugenie, hoping she was faring as well as could be expected. He was guilt-ridden he had yet to find her. When he did find her, he would make an offer for her hand. He cursed himself that it had taken something like this to get him to see what his actual feelings for her were.

He loved her, and that's all there was to it. He had

for years, but had resisted, and now he was ready to step up for his father. But first they must find her. Find the duke, and they'd find her. That is unless she'd managed to find a way to escape the old duke.

"Are you still in there?" he heard Radstock say.

"What's the rush?"

"None, other than I'm hungry enough to eat an entire cow."

Trent snorted. "Your love of food is unmatched. If you don't slow down, you'll end up looking like your father."

"God forbid! What I'm saying is we haven't had a decent meal in days. Why not go out and enjoy a good meal. Perhaps a steak."

"Alright, alright. Let me finish in peace, and we'll go find you a steak."

He heard his friend chuckle. "Excellent."

Trent finished bathing, shaving, and dressing before rejoining Radstock. He hadn't given it too much thought, but a good meal might help his attitude as he was getting quite surly from their inability to find Eugenie.

Little did he know that would all change soon.

CHAPTER 11

rent and Radstock were walking back to the hotel after enjoying a nice, leisurely meal. Two thick steaks with red wine had more than filled them up after going days with meager meals. Radstock elbowed him, causing him to look up. Standing not twenty feet from him, staring at him and Radstock in disbelief, were Lady Eugenie and a young man.

"Lady Eugenie?" he murmured as he picked up his pace.

"Trent? What on earth are you doing here in Leicester?"

He took her hands and squeezed them. "Looking for you. Radstock and I have been desperately searching for you since Northshire abducted you at the theater." He looked pensively at the young man. "Who is this?"

"You've been looking for me?" she asked, turning to the young man. "This is Thomas. He helped me escape the duke."

"Thomas, I'll never be able to thank you enough for rescuing Lady Eugenie. Were you employed by Northshire?"

"I was a groom and sometimes footman for the duke, my lord."

"Trent. . ."

Instead, he interrupted, knowing where she was going with the conversation. She was concerned about what would happen to the young man. "Thomas, why don't you go with Lord Radstock. He'll see you get a hot meal and arrange a place for you to sleep. We can talk again later, after you've rested."

"Thank you, my lord," Thomas replied as Radstock guided the boy to the hotel.

Trent turned back to Eugenie. She was still wearing the same gown she had been wearing that night at the theater. "Come, let's get you a hot meal and a bath. I'll see if some clothes can't be found for you."

"I am quite hungry. Thomas and I have been traveling trying to find a village or town so we could head back toward London. We were afraid to stay on the main road, afraid the duke's men would find us."

He guided her toward the hotel door. "You're okay, aren't you? The duke or his men didn't hurt you, did they?"

"I'm fine, Trent. Just cold and hungry."

Once inside the hotel, he approached the front desk and explained their predicament. The clerk eyed Eugenie with a raised brow but went about his business. He promised a hot meal would be delivered to the suite, and a seamstress would be called upon to help clothe Lady Eugenie.

He led her up the stairs to the suite he and Radstock had procured. "Come, I'll show you to the bathing chamber. I'm sure you'd like a good soak before anything else."

"I would, and thank you, Trent."

"No need to thank me, Eugenie."

Suddenly she wrapped her arms around his neck and kissed him. "Yes, there is. You never gave up looking for me. For that I'll be eternally grateful."

All of Trent's self-control flew out the window as he reclaimed her lips, kissing her deeply. He knew his feelings for her were there. They'd shared so much. Now that he had her back, he wasn't about to let her go.

Suddenly, he pulled away. "Come, bathe first, then you can tell me everything."

"Of course," she replied.

He showed her the bathing chamber, going so far as to start the water for her. "There's a dressing gown on the back of the door. You can wear it until a dressmaker brings you something more appropriate."

She nodded, gathering up soap and towels. "Thank you, Trent. I can manage from here."

He hadn't realized he'd been staring. She was beautiful, even disheveled as she was from her ordeal. "Would you like a glass of brandy or wine?"

She shook her head. "I'll wait until I eat. I'm afraid I'd fall asleep if I drank something now."

Trent closed the door behind her and walked to the table which held several decanters of various liquors. He poured himself a brandy, looking up as Radstock came into the room. He walked over to a chair and sat.

"I saw to the boy. He'll get a hot meal and a place to sleep. I told him you'd like to speak with him, that we both would about the duke and his possible whereabouts."

"He didn't give you any indication as to where that might have been?"

Radstock nodded. "He said something about a hunting lodge the duke owned. Said they'd been there to get out of the rain and to get the duke's fancy carriage off the road." He paused. "It was near the Unicorn."

"I knew it!"

"We'll find out more in the morning. He knows he can't go back to Northshire, so I mentioned to him not to worry. That he'd have employment either with you or me. I figure it's the least we can do."

"I couldn't agree more. I'm sure Lady Eugenie would have approached me on that matter."

"How is she?"

"Right now, cold, tired, and hungry."

"No need to rush her. She's been through a traumatic ordeal. Best let her speak in her own time."

"I agree. I'll send word to her father that she's been found."

"You could take the train back. Put that black beast of yours in a stable car."

"I'll consider it."

"We could be back in London in no time."

A knock on the door revealed a local dressmaker and two of her seamstresses. They carried what appeared to be everything Eugenie might need. He directed the ladies to the bathing chamber after telling her he was going to meet Radstock downstairs.

Radstock was seated on a gold couch enjoying a brandy. Trent sat in an overstuffed chair near his friend.

"Got run out?"

"Yes, it shouldn't take long the dressmaker told me. I asked her to make sure she had at least two changes. That'll get her back to London."

Radstock nodded. "When do you wish to leave? Tomorrow?"

"I thought we'd see if either her father or mine responds to my telegrams first. Why, did you wish to go visit your aunt?"

"No, that certainly isn't something I have to do."

A footman brought Trent a brandy. He sniffed the amber liquid before swirling it and taking a long sip. "Don't feel you're obliged to go back to London with me."

The corner of Radstock's mouth turned upward. "I hardly have the attire to spend any more than a day visit, and you know I'm not about to embarrass myself."

"There are two trains to London. We'll take the later one if we hear from London. If we don't, we'll wait and leave the morning after."

"I can't imagine your father not responding."

"True."

This time Radstock took a swallow of his brandy, polishing off the contents. "So what of you and the Lady Eugenie? Are you going to make an offer for her now?"

"Yes. I thought I'd discuss the matter with her before we head back to London."

"I guess congratulations are in order," Radstock said.

"Let's wait until I've had a chance to talk to her and then offer for her."

"I doubt you'll get much of an argument from her since both fathers were pressuring you to ask her," he said, sitting back. "By the way, I got myself a room. I don't think Lady Eugenie needs any more scandal, and sharing a suite with two gentlemen might set tongues wagging. No matter how innocent."

"Thank you. The matter had yet to cross my mind."

"Will you go live at Trent Manor?"

"Yes, after we marry. When we're not in London of course."

Radstock motioned to the footman to bring two more brandies. "That was a smart move, purchasing that estate."

"Yes, well, the house that I received is crumbling. Trent Manor is one of the finest homes I've seen in quite some time."

"That it is, and it keeps you out of your father's line of sight."

"Another reason for me purchasing the property. By

combining the two, it should turn a lucrative profit within a year or two."

"Sounds like you've got things planned through."

"That is what I'm hoping, my friend," Trent replied. "Now we must find someone for you."

"Don't bother. I can find my own wife."

Trent laughed. "Right. I recall saying the exact same thing."

One of the managers came up to them. A portly, older gentleman with a thick head of hair. "Mrs. Wiggins is finished with Lady Hamilton. She said she will send the bill over first thing in the morning."

"Thank you. Go ahead and have dinner sent up to my suite. I'm sure she's more than ready for a good hot meal."

"As you wish, my lord." The man bowed and walked back to another part of the lobby.

Radstock rose. "I'm going to check on the horses. I'll see you in the morning. We'll meet in the dining room. Perhaps your father will have sent word by then."

Trent polished off his brandy and set the glass down as he stood up. "In the morning, then."

He watched his friend walk off before glancing at the staircase leading to the guest rooms. It was time to see Eugenie, spend some time with her, and perhaps learn in greater detail exactly what had happened to her during her disappearance.

Trent took the stairs two at a time and strode down the hall to the double doors of the suite. He knocked before letting himself in. Eugenie was nowhere to be found. Probably fussing over some little detail, he mused.

He walked around the room nervously. Why was he so nervous over seeing her alone? It might be the first time in a while that they'd been alone, but that was another time. He paced around the room, waiting. He resisted the urge to pour himself a brandy, telling himself he needed to keep a sharp mind.

She walked through the door to one of the bedchambers dressed in a dove gray dress, trimmed in a dark shade of pink. Her hair was swept up off her neck. She was breathtakingly beautiful. She was so perfect. The dressmaker had worked wonders with whatever she had in stock.

Eugenie smiled as she neared. "Hard to believe I'm the same woman who entered this suite a couple of hours ago."

"You look magnificent," he said as he kissed the back of her hand. "Dinner should be here shortly. I'm sure you're hungry."

"I am. Though Northshire fed me, it was meager, simple fare," she replied. "Has he been found?"

He shook his head. "I haven't heard. It may be something we wait on until we return to London. I'm sure he's mortified knowing you escaped and haven't been caught."

"Even if my father doesn't press charges, he won't be welcome in London for quite a while, I'm sure."

"I have to agree. He'll probably hide at one of his lesser estates. I'm just happy to have you back."

"You and Radstock searched for me?"

"Yes, though we did split up at first. We were about to head to London to see if we couldn't get extra help. We knew Northshire had to be close by; we just were unable to find him."

"Well, it all worked out in the end."

"So far, yes," Trent replied. "Would you care for a glass of wine now?"

"Yes, I think I would."

"Excellent. Your dinner should be here momentarily. I thought you'd prefer to eat here rather than the restaurant with all the noise."

"Dear Trent, you're always so thoughtful."

He nodded and poured a glass of wine for her. "You've been through a terrible ordeal."

"I think the worst part was the fact I was kept where I couldn't tell if it were day or night. At the cottage, the room I was in had no windows."

"The duke, how did he treat you?"

"For the most part okay," she replied. "He was determined he was going to marry me."

"Evidently, he's in serious debt. Your dowry would make him flush again."

She took a sip of wine. "I figured it had to be something like that."

Trent wanted to know more without upsetting her. "Did he mention what his plans were? Was he going to take you to Gretna Green?"

"No, actually he wasn't. Said he had something else in mind, that he knew someone who'd marry us."

"That's behind you. I've sent word to your father. We'll leave for London tomorrow or the day after."

"I'm ready to get back."

A knock at the door told Trent Eugenie's dinner had arrived. He opened the door to a young man who placed everything on a small dining table in one corner of the room.

"Roast chicken," she said as she lifted the lid from the plate and sat down.

"If that's not to your liking, I can have something else sent."

"It looks and smells simply wonderful, Trent. Probably the best thing I've had to eat since I left London."

He nodded and let her begin to eat. He poured himself a whiskey and another wine for her and placed the wine on the table.

"Please, sit with me."

"If you're sure. . ."

"Trent, we're sharing this suite tonight. We've done a lot more that wouldn't be thought proper in the past. Don't turn shy on me now."

He smiled. "Trust me, that will never happen. Not with you." He sat across from her, setting his whiskey on the table.

"Good, because I fear I wouldn't like some new, quieter Trent," she replied as she cut a piece of chicken. "What's on your mind?"

"Just thankful you're safe."

She chewed thoughtfully. "And?"

"And what?"

"I know you, my lord. Better than most. I can tell when something weighs on your mind. Cough it up; what's got you thinking so seriously?"

It was too soon. He didn't want to speak of marriage with her quite yet. She'd been through much the past days.

"There is nothing other than what I've told you. I'm thankful you're safe."

"You were worried about me?"

"Yes, yes. There I've said it. I was worried about you; are you happy?" He swallowed his whiskey and put the glass back on the table hard.

She gazed at him demurely. "Thank you, Trent," she said.

EUGENIE FOUND herself staring at the ceiling of her bedchamber a short time later. Truth be known, she was exhausted from all that had happened the past week. She also felt it hard to be in such close proximity to Trent, and she had an idea he felt the same. He was never at a loss for words, but tonight he seemed to be struggling to find the right words. As though he were holding back.

He was expecting word back from his father, or even hers, but told her either way they would leave for London tomorrow, taking the later train. She was anxious to get back to her life, but a part of her wanted to stay, stay far away from London and society with Trent.

Trent was trying to be a gentleman. She had been through a lot after all, and he understood that and was respecting her. But something hung in the air, something she was having a hard time describing. It wasn't entirely lust, but it was something that came from deep inside her. It was as though she had an itch that needed to be scratched.

Finally, she threw back the covers and sat up. This was ridiculous. They were two grown people who'd known each other almost all their lives. The pair had shared moments so intimate she would have been declared ruined if they'd been caught. Now here they were staying together in a hotel suite with only doors separating them.

She marched out of her bedchamber, and when she came to Trent's, she pushed open the door and went inside. Surprisingly, he was sitting in front of the fire looking into the flames. He turned upon seeing her standing there dressed in nothing more than a night gown.

"Are you having trouble sleeping?" he asked, jerking his eyes back to the fire.

"Yes."

"Perhaps a brandy would help."

"I can think of something else that would help even more than brandy," she said quietly.

She neared and sat squarely on his lap and kissed him on the lips. It was a bold move on her part, but Eugenie knew of no other way to express her desires other than showing Trent what she wanted, required of him.

Eugenie let him take over, the gentle intrusion of his tongue sending chills through her. With an unspoken language of greed, tenderness, and heat, the kiss turned into something deeper. She hungered for him, having wanted this for a long time. He pulled her closer, as though he were trying to protect her and keep her safe. She moaned softly, clinging to him.

"Eugenie..." he rasped.

"Trent, I need you."

He crushed his mouth against hers and kissed her deeply once more. "Eugenie, you don't know what you ask."

"I do. I know exactly of what I ask, Trent. Please, make love to me. Make me yours."

Her mouth shaped to his, making it a much needed reflex. He grunted as she pushed herself closer.

He untied the little bow that kept her nightgown closed and loosened it with his forefinger. It fell away, just slightly over her shoulders. Eugenie felt the back of his knuckle brush against her breast, making it difficult for her to breathe from the rush of excitement. His fingers then lifted the firm, soft breast as his head lowered. She gasped and trembled as he took the rosy tip in his mouth and tugged it until it was stiff.

He stopped and gazed up at her. "I must stop now, Eugenie."

"No, Trent." She sat on his lap, legs spread for him.

He groaned.

She felt her muscles tighten as she realized his hand was making its way to her thigh. He tightened his hold on her back as his thumb slid farther, circling the edge of her silky patch of dark hair. His fingers played between her thighs. He rubbed each inner lip with his forefinger and thumb. She whimpered, nudging her sex to his palm. Never touching the swollen bud, he massaged the plump hood above it.

Eugenie gasped, writhing under his touch. "Please, Trent."

He caressed her until he felt her wetness. He stroked the entrance to her body and inserted a fingertip. He murmured as he worked deeper. She went motionless as he worked deeper.

"Relax, my love."

Her body tightened around his finger. He covered her mouth with his. She was wet, and his finger began a gentle nudging. His cock was excruciatingly hard as it pressed against her. As much as she tried to hurry him, he kept building her pleasure.

She wanted everything and moaned as he continued slowly and precisely. "More. . ." she whispered.

The pleasure built, and he covered her mouth with his as she soared to new heights she'd never known.

"There's no going back if we continue."

"Shut up Trent, and make love to me."

And so, he lifted her off his lap and carried her to his bed. He gently laid her in the middle of the mattress and began to undress himself.

Leaning over her, he kissed the side of her neck and lightly nipped at her skin. His hand slid over her body, stroking. She was pressed against his length.

Reaching between them, he adjusted the angle of his erect cock, rubbing the hard head against the apex between her thighs. She tensed, unsure what came next. He didn't push hard, just invaded her with his hardened cock.

She squirmed at his wicked caresses. Her feminine passage stretched, the intrusion wide. He was slow in his movements, letting her body accept him, his fingers dancing over the folds of her sex. He teased her unmercifully.

"Breathe, love. Breathe," he whispered.

She gasped as her body arched, stretched over his cock. "Trent!" she called out as her pleasure crested.

"Being inside you. . .I never thought I could feel this way. So complete," he gasped. His breath stopped as his release caught up with him and filled her. He shuddered, then lay on top of her, his body still pulsing from their release.

"You do know we must marry now," he said as they lay in each other's arms. "I'll offer for you when we return, but that's merely a formality."

"Really?"

"You know we must. You could be with child," he replied.

"Oh, well, I suppose that's reason enough. You realize you haven't asked me."

He pulled her closer. "I thought I did just now when we made love."

"You wicked, wicked man. Taking advantage of an innocent like me."

"If you want to be truthful, you lost your innocence with me years ago," he replied as he nuzzled at her neck.

"Don't flatter yourself," she said smugly.

He kissed her again, holding her close. Sleep crept up on them, and they slept until the early light of dawn.

CHAPTER 12

*R*adstock joined Trent and Eugenie as they enjoyed a leisurely breakfast the following morning. The day was overcast but pleasant. Better than the rain that had plagued them just a few days ago.

"Good morning, Lady Eugenie," Radstock said.

"Good morning," she replied with a smile.

He sat across from both of them. "Have you heard from your father or Lady Eugenie's yet?"

Trent nodded. "I received word from my father this morning. He said he'd go see Lady Eugenie's father himself."

"So, we head back to London? Today?"

"Yes, but don't feel obligated if you need to visit your aunt and cousin."

Radstock shook his head. "I would rather help with the horses, settling them in for the train ride back to London."

"Very well. I mean to find Thomas and see if he'd like to work in one of my stables. If he's willing, would you see him back to London and settled in?"

"Better than that. I'll have him stay with my grooms until you have Lady Eugenie settled back with her family."

"That's very kind, my lord," Eugenie said as she set down her cup of tea.

"It's no problem."

"I hope you are well rested, Lady Eugenie. The journey aboard the train is long, but far quicker than the way you went."

"I had my first decent night's sleep since this whole ordeal occurred. Thank you for asking."

Radstock rose to his full height. "If you'll excuse me, I'm going to find Thomas to ready the horses. I shall see the two of you at the train station."

Trent said nothing for a few moments, cutting a piece of sausage on his plate. "I hope you're in agreement, but I thought when I speak with your father to ask for you, I'll make it clear we don't wish a long betrothal. If that suits you."

"Absolutely. I want nothing more than to marry you and begin a new life as your marchioness. I think immediate family, perhaps a few very close friends is plenty."

"With a wedding breakfast before we leave for my estate in the country. I know you'll love it there."

"I've heard great things about the house, how beautiful it is."

He smiled. "Yes, and I'm glad I purchased it."

"Then that's settled."

"I'll see about getting a special license tomorrow."

She arched a brow in his direction. "Hopefully, my father will approve."

"I'm sure he will, after all our parents have wanted this match for a very long time."

THE DUKE and Duchess of Brandon were anxiously waiting in the drawing room of their London residence, along with Trent's own parents, the Duke and Duchess of Marlborough. Eugenie took in a deep breath as her mother and father both embraced her.

Her own father was more emotional that she thought she'd ever seen him. Tears formed in his light blue eyes as he laid eyes on his daughter.

"Thank goodness you are safe, daughter," he said with some emotion cracking his voice as he turned to Trent, who was standing with his own parents. "I'm forever in your debt for returning my daughter to her mother and me; thank you."

Trent merely nodded his head, unsure if there were any words that were appropriate at a time such as this.

After the duke let go of his daughter, her mother and Trent's fussed over her like two possessive mother hens.

Brandon took the lead.

"Come, gentlemen. Let's retire to my study. I believe there is much to discuss that isn't for women's fair ears."

Which meant Brandon was in need of a whiskey to get control of his emotions. Trent followed both older men to the duke's study where the duke went straight to a crystal decanter sitting on the edge of his massive oak desk. He picked it up and poured three glasses before handing one to each man.

A toast was made and small talk ensued. Trent realized he was going to have to act now, even with his father present.

"There is a matter I wish to discuss regarding Lady Eugenie," he said softly.

"Yes, go on. I pray it isn't regarding her time with Northshire. I plan on having him brought up on charges for abducting my daughter."

"No, though I agree with you one hundred percent on having him brought up on charges," Trent replied.

"No, this is about Lady Eugenie's and my future, Your Grace. I should like to ask for your daughter."

A faint smile crossed Brandon's face as he took in the news. "That's splendid news."

His father clapped him on the back. "Yes, that's wonderful news, Trent."

"When did my daughter agree to a marriage with you?" Brandon inquired.

"We had many a long talk after I found her. I believe her abduction opened her eyes."

He wasn't sure Brandon was actually buying into his story, which wasn't entirely all fiction. He had to be careful so the duke didn't figure out he'd bedded Brandon's daughter.

"I'm sure it did," Brandon replied.

"I'm applying for a special license tomorrow. Lady Eugenie and I feel it best if we wed as quickly as possible."

"Pray tell why?"

Trent carefully contemplated his answer. "People talk, and I'm sure there will be a lot of it once news of her release comes out. I mean to make her my wife. I can protect her that way."

"Very well. You have my permission. I'll have the papers ready for you in the morning."

"Thank you, Your Grace."

"I'm just happy the two of you have come to some sort of agreement."

"One last thing. Under the circumstances, Eugenie does not wish to have a large wedding. Instead, something simple with just immediate family and friends."

"Consider it done. I'll speak with her mother myself."

Trent nodded. "If you gentlemen will excuse me. It's been a long journey and ordeal. I should like to retire to my home."

"Yes, by all means," Brandon said. "You must be exhausted from all that has happened."

He nodded to his father before leaving. "I'll leave you gentlemen. I'll see you in the morning, Your Grace."

"Very well," Brandon replied. "Make sure you let my daughter know you're leaving." The duke smiled.

Trent nodded to both older gentlemen, placed his glass down on the duke's desk, and walked out of the room. He headed toward the drawing room. It would be the last time he'd see Lady Eugenie until tomorrow, and he needed one more look.

She and both duchesses were sitting near the windows drinking tea. Whatever they were discussing, it was obvious it was of a feminine nature as upon seeing him, they refrained from any talk.

"Ladies. I just wanted to say goodbye. I'm heading to my townhouse." He glanced lovingly at Eugenie. "We'll talk again tomorrow."

"We will?"

"Yes, there's a matter your father and I have to tend to."

"Until tomorrow, my lord," she said with a smile.

He quit the room and headed toward his carriage. He climbed in and leaned back. She certainly had gotten under his skin. Never had he even considered a woman as fine as Eugenie or any other woman for his bride. Though their fathers had tried pushing a union for the sake of business and prestige, Eugenie and he were in fact falling deeply in love.

Their wedding couldn't come soon enough. After procuring the special license tomorrow, he would sit down with Eugenie and set a date. Sometime within a fortnight. He was anxious to take her to the privacy of his Gloucestershire estate. He wanted not to just share its splendor with her; Trent wanted nothing more than to sequester the two of them in his bedchamber and discover all of each other. From their couplings in the hotel, Trent was convinced Eugenie may well have a submissive side. He'd always kept a certain side of his sexual appetite private, only partaking at a certain brothel he and a few of his friends frequented. He could easily see Eugenie spread out for him in the middle of his bed, ripe for teaching.

Why he thought of this now, he had no idea. There hadn't been time for such foolishness, but having had Eugenie had made him reconsider his options.

His thoughts were quickly interrupted by the cease in the swaying of the carriage. He was home, at least in London, but none the less home, and he was never happier to be home.

131

CHAPTER 13

hree days later the Marquess of Trent and the Lady Eugenie were married in the drawing room of her parent's London home. The only guests were the groom's long-time friend, Viscount Radstock and his own betrothed, the Lady Lucinda. Also present were the Lady Eugenie's childhood friend, Helena Conley, Countess of Dover and her husband, the Earl of Dover.

Eugenie chose to wear a beaded ivory silk gown. Her reddish-blond hair was swept up off her neck in a fashionable style. She had chosen the gown for its elegance. Her mother had fussed about it at first while at the modiste but quickly changed her mind when she realized her daughter might indeed wear it to her wedding.

She had chosen her wardrobe with great care when packing her things to go with her to Trent's country estate. The rest would be sent to their London home, at least temporarily. Now married, she would have reason for a new wardrobe. She was becoming a marchioness.

Her hand shook slightly as she signed the marriage papers, perfectly normal for most brides. But she wasn't just any bride. For years she'd fought marriage, and through it all, Trent had been the one constant in her life. He proved himself worthy and forever changed her mind on the institution of marriage. She and Trent would be happy married, and with any luck, she would one day soon present him with an heir.

Eugenie took her husband's hand as he led her back to their guests. Husband. What a strange word. It had at one time conjured up all sorts of images she wanted no part of. Now, it rolled off the tongue with ease.

An elaborate wedding breakfast was waiting to be served, as everyone made their way to the dining room. They would dine on freshly caught Scottish salmon, roast goose, and other delicacies. There had even been time for a wedding cake to be made, which the guests would be sent home with, and Eugenie knew some would be sent with them.

Toasts were made with the finest champagne her father owned. Everyone was in awe as each course was presented to the bride and groom. Eugenie was amazed by what her mother's staff had been able to make given the schedule they'd had to work with.

She nervously glanced at her husband. He caught her and leaned over to say something to her.

"If you need to change, you might want to do so now," he whispered.

"I'd like to wear my wedding gown a while longer," she replied in a whisper.

"Very well. It's about time we leave."

She nodded. "I believe I'll freshen up and join you in the grand hall in say about fifteen minutes."

"I'll count the minutes. I can't wait for us to be on our way, for you to see your new home."

She rose and Trent helped her. Much champagne had been consumed, and she was feeling the effects even though she had partaken in only two glasses. She made her way upstairs for a few moments of privacy and to ready herself for the journey.

Her mother had tried to have a talk with her on what to expect on her wedding night. It was a topic the duchess was not comfortable speaking about. Eugenie, however, sensing her mother's discomfort, had thanked her mother and assured her everything would be fine. She would get through the first night, and afterwards, everything would be easier. She'd also sensed that her parent's marriage was not a loveless marriage, but one where love was not shared any longer in the marital bed. In fact, she walked away wondering if her mother had ever enjoyed it or if it had merely been something she was required to submit to as a wife. Her father had always kept a mistress, at least Eugenie thought he had. He was, after all, a man, and having a wife who found the marriage bed distasteful, she couldn't fault her father if he looked elsewhere to soothe his needs. Hopefully, it would never be like that for Trent and her. It was the one part she actually was looking forward to.

She looked at her lady's maid, Mona, who would be accompanying her to her new home, though in a separate carriage. "Are you ready to begin our new life, Mona?"

"Yes, my lady."

"Then let us depart for our new home. The marquess tells me it's quite something to behold. My father has said as much himself."

The maid bobbed, picked up the last of Eugenie's belongings, and stuffed them into a bag as Eugenie left her childhood bedchamber for the very last time.

THE CARRIAGE TURNED onto the oak lined drive leading to Trent Manor. Eugenie stared out the carriage window, straining for a glimpse of her new home. Finally, the circular drive came into view with the majestic manor house on the other side.

The structure made of ashlar blocks towered three stories. It was magnificent just like Trent had said it was. She could immediately see why he'd purchased the estate. Even located next to the original Marquess of Trent's home, this was far from the crumbling decay of the former.

"What do you think, wife?" she heard Trent's voice rumble in the background.

"It's spectacular. It's everything you said it was. I can see why you love spending time here."

The carriage door opened, and the steps lowered. Trent stepped out first and then offered his hand to his bride.

"Welcome home," he said.

She was holding on to his hand, still looking up at the manor's front facade in wonderment. The outside touted neo-classical decorations, part of what made it unique. Suddenly, as though she recalled where she was, she diverted her attention back to Trent.

"I cannot wait to discover every nook and cranny of this magnificent house."

He smiled. "There will be lots of time for that. First, however, Fitzsimmons and Mrs. Gibbons are waiting to meet you and introduce you to the rest of the staff."

She smiled and placed her hand on his arm as he led her to the front door where he made introductions.

"May I introduce Fitzsimmons. He's the butler here at Trent Manor and has been for many years. He and Mrs. Gibbons came with the place when I purchased it."

She smiled at both of the older staff members. "Mrs. Gibbons, I take it you're the housekeeper?"

"Yes, my lady."

"What of the remainder of the staff? Are they new,

or are there any who came with the house when my husband purchased it?"

"There are a few. By the time Lord Trent purchased the property, the house and grounds were maintained by a skeleton staff."

"I see," Eugenie replied. "Perhaps in the next days we can go over the household and decide if there's need for more staff."

"Yes, my lady."

The staff seemed to disappear as Trent continued leading them inside. The grand hall's floor was done in grey and white marble and was open to the roof. It was indeed grand. The master staircase was broken into two. Depending on which side of the upper rooms one wanted to go to, there was a staircase leading and welcoming guests.

Eugenie was in awe. Never had she seen anything so spectacular, except perhaps in a palace.

"I cannot imagine someone not wishing to keep this," she muttered.

Trent gestured to one side. "There's a portrait gallery over there. It's still being worked on, adding portraits I've had brought from the previous Trent Manor. Come, let me show you to the drawing room. We can have tea while your lady's maid unpacks your belongings."

"I would like that as I'm quite parched."

He led her up the right staircase and led her to a magnificent blue and cream drawing room. The room was unlike any Eugenie had seen before. Certainly, what her parents had was superb, Trent's parents, too, but this—this was elegant. Someone had put a lot of thought and attention into the detail of the color scheme, wall coverings, and floor, which was an intricate wood pattern covered by blue and gold tapestry rugs. The furniture was relatively new, done in the same shades of blue, cream, and gold.

Eugenie felt as though she were living in a dream. "This is so elegant," she said. "Is the rest of the house as beautiful as this room?"

"Yes, I'm afraid so," he mocked.

"Trent, you have no idea what you have here."

He shook his head. "I know exactly what I have here in Trent Manor. The house is furnished in the manner of this room. There is a collection of Ming porcelain throughout the house, along with some artwork painted by some of the best."

"I can't wait to discover it all."

"Come, tea should be here momentarily," he said, leading her to a gold settee.

Eugenie sat next to him and looked nervously at him. There was an air of electricity between them, and for now, it was as though they had to let society dictate how they behaved, but she knew once they were in the privacy of his bed chambers, all bets were off.

She felt his finger as he traced it down the side of her face to her jawbone before it finally rested on the pulse point on her neck. "Your skin is flushed, and your pulse races. Are you nervous, my dear?"

Yes. Yes.

"Yes," she said softly.

He smiled slightly. "And why are you nervous? It's not as if we haven't been together before."

She knew she was under his spell, powerless to turn away. "I. . .I don't know. I guess I'm just overwhelmed. So much has happened today."

"Don't overthink things, angel." He brought his lips closer, pressing them onto her neck. Trent kissed where her pulse pounded, his tongue licking her skin.

"I'm trying not to, but you're making it very difficult, Trent."

There was a knock on the drawing room door, and Trent straightened up, smiling wickedly and all-knowing at her. Tea was brought in and the service placed on the table before them. Eugenie found herself suddenly not thirsty

No, what she was thirsty for was more of what Trent was wanting to show her. She glanced at him through hooded eyes as she prepared tea for each of them. He was a gorgeous man; the natural part of his inky black hair, which was now tousled, and those gorgeous piercing deep blue eyes. He was an Adonis among men, and she was just beginning to memorize every inch of his muscular body.

She passed him the cup of tea before sitting back with hers. She sipped and said nothing, but then neither of them spoke. It was an awkward moment for them both. Trent was still looking at her, his gaze never leaving hers. What could he be thinking?

He took a polite sip and smiled before placing the cup into its saucer. "Shall I show you to our chambers?"

Our chambers? She wondered what he meant by that. Mostly couples had their own rooms, the ladies' connecting to the men's with a door. Was this what he meant?

"Yeeesss," she replied.

He helped her to her feet and held her close for a moment as he pressed his erection into her stomach. It was then she understood. They were now man and wife; nothing they did together in the privacy of their bed or beyond was now off limits. Anything was possible, and with that freedom, Eugenie wanted it all. She wanted him to take her from the semi-shy virgin she'd been in Leicester to the smoldering lover she wished to become.

The bedchamber of the marquess was done in varying shades of green, not unlike the drawing room.

As she looked about the room, she observed how masculine the room was. It was also neat and organized. Everything had its place.

Trent walked over to the closed door which connected both rooms. "Would you care to freshen up?"

She nodded shyly. "Yes, thank you."

"I'll leave the door open."

"Thank you. I shan't be but a few minutes, Trent."

"I'll be at my desk."

She disappeared into the inner sanctum of the marchioness's private rooms. They were done in shades of pale pink and deep rose. Quickly and quietly she took care of her own needs and looked around for her lady's maid, who was nowhere to be found. The older woman was usually hovering; today she had all but disappeared, probably not imagining her mistress would need her before dinner.

It meant she could not change without help. Trent would probably love the idea of being asked to unlace her corset. She sat down and looked into the mirror as she took the pins from her hair and brushed it. It was the one thing she could do herself.

Eugenie rejoined Trent, who was as he'd told her he would be, sitting at a writing desk, looking over papers.

"I'm afraid my lady's maid is nowhere to be found. She probably is getting settled in herself."

He stood and walked over to join her. "It's all right, Eugenie." He locked the door leading to her room. Trent led her to his bedchamber and began to unlace her dress with experienced fingers. There was no doubt Trent knew what he was doing.

She felt his lips as he slowly caressed her skin with his heat. How could she crave him so much? There had always been this magnetic force between them. It was as though she were addicted to him.

Her dress fell to the floor, leaving her clad only in

her stockings, garters, and undergarments, all of which he took great pleasure in removing. He picked her up and spread her in the middle of the mattress; his eyes flared as he watched her every movement as he removed his own clothes.

He mounted her, gripping her shins and bending her at the knees to make his way to her apex. Eugenie felt herself blush. Never had she felt so exposed before. He was looking her over.

Then he sank his cock into her. This was going to be his claiming of her, showing her she was his wife and lover. She was no one else's but Trent's. He pounded as far as he could, taking her in deep, hard strokes.

Eugenie began to feel something inside of herself, her body needing, wanting more as she succumbed to the intensity of the orgasm he gave her as she struggled to hold on to reality.

"Treennnt," she heard herself call out as she realized he came with her. He thrust hard and deep and finally shuddered into her for the final few times. She could feel his cock jerking inside her, her inner muscles clutching him.

For a moment, they both lay there. Trent on top of her, both silent, their breathing the only thing that was heard.

"I'm sorry," he said suddenly as he balanced on his elbows, looking down at her.

"What do you feel sorry for?"

"I, uh, I don't know what came over me. I just felt the urge to take you, make you mine. If that makes sense to you."

She stared up at him, their eyes locked. "Yes, I think it does."

He rolled off of her and tucked her against his body. "I promise to be more thoughtful in the future."

"I have no doubt you will be," she replied.

She felt his hands wander. The man certainly could turn it on and off at will. A gentleman for one moment, a demanding lover the next. He took a nipple in between his teeth and softly bit down. The combination of teeth and his beard pricking her skin sent her to another realm.

He stared down at her, his dark hair falling forward. He could be dangerous and dominant if he wanted to be, and he knew it. He sucked at one of her nipples again until it was hard. His mouth pulled away from her breasts and moved down her body. When he reached his intended destination, he spread her legs wide as he dipped his mouth to her cunt. That same feeling began to overcome her. But rather than helping her finish whatever this was he'd started, he stopped and sat, his hard cock in his hand as he pulled it.

"Open your mouth. I want to teach you what pleases me."

Eyes wide open, Eugenie stared but accepted him as he buried his cock deep in her mouth. He began to push, then withdraw his cock in slow, precise movements. It was natural, a part of their essence. She found her tongue darting over his hardness.

When he withdrew, he lay her on her back and entered her. This time she met him stroke for stroke as he drilled into her. She finally trembled beneath him as her eyes widened. Her back arched to take him deeper as he called out her name before his cock spilled his seed deep inside her. She called out his name as she climaxed.

"Trent?" she finally said as she ran her soft hand across his chest.

"Yes?"

"Will it always be like this?"

He kissed the top of her head. "God, I hope so."

CHAPTER 14

The sun peeked through the bedchamber windows the following morning. Trent gazed lovingly at his bride, who lay blissfully asleep next to him. He hated to wake her, but the day called, and he wanted to show her the estate, and knowing how much she loved to ride, what better way than by horseback.

"Good morning, my love."

She stirred, then stretched and yawned. "Good morning. What time is it?"

"After eight. I thought after breakfast you might like to take a ride and see the estate."

"That sounds splendid. I am hungry. I don't think we barely touched dinner last night," she said.

"No, we were rather preoccupied last night."

She sat up and kissed him. "I'm going to take a quick bath and dress. Shall I meet you here? I'm afraid I don't know where anything is."

"Here will be just fine," he replied. "Don't bathe on my account. I love the smell of us on you."

"Ewwww. I'm sorry, but I need a bath, Lord Trent."

"As you wish, Lady Trent. I'm sure you don't need me to show you the way to your bathing chamber. Not that I wouldn't be happy to do so."

She rolled off the bed, grabbing the sheet to cover herself, blushing as she did. Trent had to smile at the gesture. Though she was comfortable with him, a shyness still remained. It wouldn't be long before Eugenie felt comfortable in every aspect of this part of their marriage.

He was sitting at the writing desk going over his correspondence that had arrived while he had been away. Normally, he would do this in his study, but since Eugenie requested for him to show her downstairs, he'd had his valet bring the mail to his door.

Trent gazed up from a letter he was reading. There she was, standing as beautiful as ever in a dark blue riding outfit. Since Eugenie only rode side saddle when forced to, he had no idea what sort of costume she might wear. Today she wore a pair of riding breeches, especially made for her. A white blouse was topped by a long split coat, which was buttoned up. She wore brown riding boots with it. She looked stunning.

"Shall we go eat, my lord?" she asked breathlessly.

Trent rose from his chair and neared her, bending to kiss her. "I'm famished, though food is not the only thing I'm hungry for."

She playfully pushed him away with one hand. "We can't have that. You need food to keep your strength, my lord."

He led her down the hall and down one level to the breakfast room. He caught her gazing at the pilasters, cornice, and parapet. Architecture had always fascinated Eugenie, and it did his heart good to see she had more than a mere enjoyment of the interior of the house. At one point, she stopped to admire some old painting left behind when he'd taken possession of the estate. A landscape painted by some Dutch master he'd been told. He knew the painting could be valuable, and he needed to go through the entire house and catalog every painting. The one he'd been given upon purchase was old and probably out of date. Eugenie might enjoy helping him on such a project.

After breakfast, they walked to the stables. Eugenie had won the heart of his two hunting dogs, Jasper and Sam, who followed her closely since they'd left the breakfast room. They circled her in excitement as she bent to study some pink and lavender flowers.

They stood hand in hand as they waited for the young stable hand to saddle both his stallion, Solomon, and a bay gelding named Stanley. The boy brought Stanley around to the mounting block where Eugenie expertly swung a leg over her mount.

He led her across the fields to the top of a small hill where they could see the vastness of not only his estate, but neighboring ones as well. The dogs followed the whole way running, sniffing for rabbits and other game.

Trent stopped to let her take in the view. "Breathtaking, isn't it?" he said.

"Oh, yes, it is."

He admired her as she sat on Stanley's back, taking it all in. Her long hair had been pulled back and blew in the breeze in tandem with the gelding's mane. She was a goddess who could ride. Perfect perfection.

"I think I need to kiss you again, wife."

"Yes, please, Lord Trent. It's been a while."

He leaned over and kissed her and breathed in her scent before breaking the kiss. They continued on walking. Needing to touch her, to kiss her again, Trent stopped and leaned over to kiss her unexpectedly.

Ominous clouds appeared out of nowhere, the sun slipping behind them. It looked as though the sky would open at any moment.

"Come, we need to head back," he said.

With the dogs racing madly alongside the horses,

they raced back to the manor house, making it back before the rain descended. As they neared the stable, the rainstorm opened up. They rode the horses into the stables and handed them over to waiting stable boys. The sound of the pounding rain hitting the roof of the stables was deafening.

They stood near the door until the rain began to soften and lighten up until it stopped, allowing them to walk back to the house.

TRENT'S COUNTRY home amazed Eugenie. Never had she seen such beauty, not only in an estate, but the house was any woman's dream. She couldn't imagine having to redecorate for years, even though Trent had told her to do whatever she wished. Every room she'd been in since arriving was perfect in her opinion, and she couldn't wait to see every remaining room in the house.

Though it was supposed to be time for just the two of them, there were still matters which needed Trent's attention. After a light luncheon, he retired to his study to meet with his estate manager. Eugenie decided to make use of her time by walking to the kitchens in search of the housekeeper. Perhaps Mrs. Gibbons could give her a quick tour of the house. They could use the time to discuss the running of such a grand house. It was a daunting task, and Eugenie had made her mind up that she would not make any changes for at least a month unless absolutely necessary.

She knew she was in the right corridor by the wonderful smells coming from the closed door at the end. Eugenie sucked in a deep breath and pushed the door open, reminding herself that she was now the lady of this grand manor.

She was a marchioness!

Everything halted when she came through the door. Kitchen maids halted in their tracks; even the cook and the girls assisting her stopped what they were doing. Everyone stood in dead silence, perhaps shocked by the sight of their marchioness visiting. Something most ladies of the manor would never do. They'd meet their cooks or housekeepers somewhere else. Never the kitchens.

"Please go back to what you were doing. I'm merely familiarizing myself with the house. I knew I was close to the kitchens by the wonderful smells."

The housekeeper, Mrs. Gibbons, came rushing forward. "My lady, is there something in particular I can help you with?"

"No, like I said, I was exploring the house. Since I'm here, you might introduce me to the cook," Eugenie replied. "There were so many faces yesterday, I can't remember Mrs. White's."

A plump middle-aged woman came forward from where she'd been stirring a pot. Her hair had once been a light shade of brown but was now sprinkled with gray. "I'm Mrs. White, my lady."

Mrs. Gibbons quickly got the staff back to work to give Eugenie and the cook time to converse, though all eyes were still on the young, new marchioness.

"Delighted to meet you, Mrs. White. I know you're terribly busy, but might you have a moment to chat?"

"Of course, my lady."

"I thought perhaps we could go over the menus for as long as you have them planned out. That way I can sample everything, and if changes need to be made, we can discuss it then."

Mrs. White nodded. "A wise decision, my lady."

"May I ask what's for dinner tonight?"

"Roasted chicken with potatoes and cod in a cream sauce."

"I look forward to it, though but I should tell you know I'm not overly fond of fish. And please don't change anything for tonight. I know my husband loves fish," Eugenie replied. "How about we meet in the morning while the duke is locked away in his study?"

"Yes, my lady."

Eugenie nodded. She didn't want to keep the woman from her duties, but it was obvious Mrs. White was quite unused to a marchioness gracing her kitchens. "Your scones are excellent. Why don't you plan on a plate with tea when we meet tomorrow?"

The woman beamed at the compliment. "I'll have them just out of the oven, my lady."

"I look forward to them. I'll let you get back to what you were doing. It was nice speaking with you, Mrs. White."

Mrs. White curtsied and went back to her stove. Eugenie smiled at Mrs. Gibbons, who was standing nearby, before Eugenie turned and left the room, satisfied with the observations she'd made. The kitchens seemed to run quite smoothly. No one standing around, everyone had a job to do and seemed to be making good use of their time.

She walked back to the grand hall and up the stairs. She wanted to find the library and music room. Trent had told her she wouldn't be disappointed in either.

Opening a closed door, she found herself in the library. Shutting the door behind her, she stood in awe at the shelves of books. Bookcases stacked from floor to ceiling, all packed with books. She neared one of the shelves and glanced at how the books were placed. It seemed to her everything on this particular shelf was about agriculture, things a duke might be interested in.

They also appeared to be in alphabetic order according to author.

With this number of books, there surely had to be a list not only of the books, but where and how things were categorized. If there weren't, there should be. It would be a daunting undertaking but was doable. She would look around or inquire with Mr. Fitzsimmons. Trent said he'd come with the estate when he purchased it, so he should have some knowledge of the contents.

She spent the next hour looking about the room, familiarizing herself with what was here. It was, like the rest of the house, tastefully furnished. A writing desk against one wall, a small table against another, perfect for playing chess or cards. Leather chairs and a couch to sit and read for hours. The floors were furnished with exquisite, richly colored Persian rugs.

Her next stop turned out to be the music room. A piano graced one portion of the room, and a harp sat in one corner. The walls were covered with a wallpaper depicting musical notes and stanzas. It matched the coverings on the furniture. Someone had gone to a lot of time and expense to have the room furnished. It must have been their favorite.

Eugenie wondered who'd owned the estate. Had they been musical or studious? Certainly, the thought put into either room wasn't just for show. Someone with great appreciation for literature and music had gone to great lengths to see that the rooms were each a paradise.

Mr. Fitzsimmons appeared as she left the music room. He was typical of most butlers. Obviously, he'd been doing it for years, quite serious, and knew everything about the workings of the estate.

"I see you found the music room, my lady," he rumbled.

"Yes, it's gorgeous. I look forward to spending time there and in the library. Tell me, do you know if there's some sort of list with the arrangement of the books?"

He nodded curtly. "Yes, I believe there is. I'll find it for you and set it out on the desk. I'm not sure how updated it is, but that wouldn't be too hard."

"Good. I was wondering if there's a study or something similar for the marchioness? I know it's unusual, but I find I don't like to be confined to my chambers for things like that. Never have."

"As a matter of fact, there is such a room. The previous lady of the house also used it extensively. If you'd like I can show it to you, my lady."

"Would you?"

"Come this way. It's quite near. The room gets the afternoon light, though it's not direct."

They continued walking until they came upon another closed door. Fitzsimmons opened it and allowed her to pass. It was obvious this was a woman's sanctuary. The room was done in pleasant shades of yellow and blue. A desk sat in front of a window overlooking gardens. The furnishings were quite feminine, probably from France; the rug she recognized as coming from China. The lighting was perfect should she want to do needlework or draw, and there was plenty of space for it.

"I do love this room," she said softly. "I can see myself spending a lot of time in here."

"Then you would like your correspondence here?"

"Yes. I'll have my lady's maid bring my needlework and sketch pads as well."

She walked around the room, looking at everything with great interest. There were a great number of paintings on the walls. Mainly flowers or landscapes where flowers were the predominate feature. Trent had mentioned wanting her to go through the house and look at all the artwork. Now she could see why.

Many tasks awaited her. Cataloging the artwork would be her first. She turned to the butler, who stood stoically. "Do you know if there is a list of all the artwork in the house?"

"I don't recall. I can't see there not being one. I'll look into it for you, my lady."

"Thank you. The marquess asked me to go through the house and catalog the artwork. There're a great number of paintings, and it would be good to know what each is, by whom, and where in the house it's located."

"I will get on it, my lady. Can I help you with anything else?"

"No, thank you, Fitzsimmons. I appreciate all your help."

He bowed curtly, the way butlers did. "Very well, my lady. On another note, where would you like luncheon served?"

"Let me check with the Marquess and see if he's going to be able to join me. The terrace would be wonderful if it's warm enough outside."

Fitzsimmons left, and Eugenie stood in front of the windows, peering out at the gardens. She noted a gardener working on trimming back a bush. She was so engrossed she didn't hear Trent enter the room.

He came up behind her, startling Eugenie. "Fitzsimmons told me where I might find you."

"Yes, he's been quite helpful."

Trent nodded. "He is. He's worked in the house since he was a boy, so he's a wealth of information when it comes to what's here. If he can't find it, it doesn't exist."

"That makes sense."

He nuzzled her neck. "What have you been up to besides becoming familiar with the house?"

"I introduced myself to the cook, and we're going to meet tomorrow. Besides that, I discovered the library and music rooms, and Fitzsimmons showed me this one."

"I see," he whispered in her ear.

Eugenie knew what he was up to, but let him continue to rub his scratchy beard across her cheek. "I asked to have our luncheon served outside on the terrace. Should we see if it's ready?"

"Very well, but afterwards, you're mine."

"Did you have something in mind, my lord? Riding again? Perhaps you have found a secluded out of the way place we could dally. Or we could stay here inside."

"I would love nothing better than to dally with my marchioness," he rasped.

"Is there somewhere quiet indoors? Somewhere the staff rarely goes?"

He laughed, a deep rumbling sound. "As a matter of fact, there is, but I'm going to save it for a rainy day. Why don't we ride after we eat? There is so much to show you, and I think you'll like the spot I have in mind."

"I'm intrigued, my lord."

He pulled away and took her hand. They walked out of the room. "I'll see horses are saddled while you see luncheon is served."

"Very well, my lord. I'll meet you on the terrace in a moment."

It didn't take Eugenie long to find a waiting footman. She told him what she required and watched as he quickly walked toward the kitchens. Turning, she began to walk to the drawing room, stopping to look at different paintings. There were so many, and she was sure each told a story. She hoped Fitzsimmons would be able to find some sort of records regarding the artwork on display in the house. Since the house wasn't old by some standards, she wondered if the art could have come from another estate.

Another item to discuss with her handsome husband. If not, and Fitzsimmons found records, it might tell a story of where pieces came from. She also needed to speak to Trent about the importance of that.

There was much to do, and she looked forward to all of it. Her time certainly wouldn't be dull here at Trent Manor. She knew Trent would have to go back to his business, and she would be left to her own devices. Tomorrow she would sit down and make herself a list of what needed her attention, inside and out. Meeting with the head gardener would be one thing. Riding and exploring the estate was something else she very much wanted to do. Trent would probably send a groom to ride with her when she did ride. At least until she was more familiar with the estate.

She was pleased to find Trent sitting at a wrought iron table on the terrace enjoying a glass of wine. Lunch had just arrived, and the footmen were busy setting it up on a table next to the house. He looked devilishly handsome. He had a noble profile, and anyone who saw him would know so. She wondered about a small scar which ran along his jawline on the left. It was old and faded, so she wondered if he'd gotten it as a young boy.

CHAPTER 15

"*J*told you marriage to my daughter would be beneficial to us all," the Duke of Brandon said.

Eugenie listened as her father, Trent, and his father, the Duke of Marlborough, spoke among themselves just outside the French doors of the terrace. Their parents had come for a day-long visit. Since they both lived nearby, Eugenie didn't have to worry about entertaining them for extended periods of time. They'd go home this evening.

But whatever this was her father spoke of was something she'd never heard before. How could marriage to her benefit anyone? Well, perhaps Trent had benefitted from the marriage to a degree. Her dowry had been very generous, but Trent had been insistent that the money be set aside for any daughters they might have.

She inched closer to the doors of the drawing room for a further listen. She was supposed to be meeting with her mother and Trent's for a tour of the house, but she'd forgotten her shawl in the drawing room. This was how she'd come to overhear the men's conversation.

She inched closer, hoping to learn more without being discovered.

"Joining our two families has made one powerful union," the Duke of Marlborough agreed.

"Your purchasing this estate and combining it with the original Marquess's land is proof of that," Brandon said.

"I purchased it because the original Marquess of Trent's home is a crumbling ruin and eyesore. If this hadn't become available, I'd be throwing money away on the other."

"Now that you've married, we can begin looking into ways we can combine our resources," Marlborough said.

"Precisely," Brandon agreed. "I think a drink is in order."

"I can take care of that," she heard Trent say.

Knowing she couldn't let him find her eavesdropping on their conversation, Eugenie quickly scurried from the room, leaving her shawl on the floor behind her. What she had just heard was new to her, and she wondered if she should ask her husband about it later.

She caught up with her mother and the Duchess of Marlborough where she'd left them in the red drawing room, which overlooked a private rose garden full of red roses in varying shades. Speaking about the subject matter she'd just heard was a conversation she just couldn't have with either woman. They were of a completely different era and left business and estate matters to their husbands' expertise.

"I took the liberty of ordering tea," her mother said as Eugenie closed the door behind her.

Before she could answer, her mother-in-law was talking about the house and furnishings. "Trent was so fortunate to have found this house, and next door to his own estate. It's so befitting the heir of the duke of Marlborough, don't you agree, Eugenie?"

Eugenie nodded. "Yes."

Her mother chimed in as well, determined not to be outdone by the other duchess in the room. "The house is so elegantly furnished. Eugenie won't have to change a thing for many years."

"Why, the artwork in the house is worth a fortune, and I know some of the furniture came from France," the Duchess of Marlborough trilled. "I hope Trent has taken inventory or has someone taking inventory of what's here."

"I'm sure he was given an inventory when he purchased the estate," Eugenie began to reply, but Fitzsimmons and a footman brought a tray with tea and plates of cakes and other sweets.

Eugenie walked across the room to a couch and chairs near the large windows and French doors so they could all enjoy the roses. The footman set the tray on the table before the two duchesses. Eugenie nodded, letting him know that was all right. She knew her mother would take over and serve tea, and she wouldn't say anything different. Her mother had always loved to entertain, garden parties and teas being among her favorites. The duchess was extremely fond of roses and was thrilled when Trent had told her Eugenie's new home had extensive rose gardens.

"Are you and Trent planning a wedding trip soon?" her mother asked.

"We have discussed waiting until next spring and going to Italy before it gets too hot."

Lady Marlborough smiled and shook her head. "You'll probably be with child by then. Traveling that far would be out of the question."

Eugenie's look must have been one of shock because

Lady Marlborough made an exaggerated gesture with her hand. "If he's anything like his father, you'll find yourself with child quickly, if you aren't already."

"Well, on the chance I'm not, Italy is where we're talking about going. Trent said Italy was one of the places he went on his grand tour and thoroughly enjoyed it."

"Don't forget France. There is so much more than just Paris," her mother chimed in.

The two duchesses immersed themselves in a conversation about France, the coastline, Provence in particular, and of course, Paris and the fashion. At least the two women were good friends; they didn't have to pretend to be polite. They'd known each other a long, long time, and Eugenie liked to refer to them as the 'double d's'.

"I've got plenty to do right here."

"You and Trent will need to think about hosting a ball or soiree when you return to London," Lady Marlborough said.

"Yes, you must," her mother agreed. "Have you given any thought to doing something here? Small, of course."

"No, Mother. This is supposed to be Trent's and my time together since we are putting off a wedding trip until next spring. A houseful of company even for a small soiree is not how either of us care to spend our evenings right now."

"Yes, you should enjoy your time together. Once you have children, things do change," Lady Marlborough said.

Eugenie wondered how the duchesses could think that having children would change a thing. Children were kept in the nursery with their nannies or nurses or governesses and tutors. Their mothers were lucky if they saw them once a day, and that was usually a scheduled time. That's how children were raised.

Eugenie had no intention once she and Trent had children to leave them entirely to a staff to raise. They would raise their children differently.

She sat and sipped her tea as she listened to the duchesses go on and on about how they thought Eugenie should manage her house.

🐎

NEVER HAD Trent been so glad to see guests leave. He was fairly sure Eugenie felt the same way. She looked spent and tired from an afternoon and evening with both of their mothers. He'd withstood all he could listening to his father and Eugenie's father drone on about what was going on politically, one of two projects they wanted to include Trent in, and finally how joining the two families made them among the most powerful in England. He'd have much rather spent a private afternoon with his bride than to listen to all that.

His father, no doubt, had been overruled by his mother. She had worn him down, wanting to see Trent's new home. She refused to believe any young couple needed more than a day after they were wed. Wedding trips were nice, but duties took preference over pleasure.

Surely it hadn't been that way for his parents, but his mother refused to talk of personal matters such as her and his father's personal life. That was between them and no one else. He knew his parents had separate bedchambers and lived a very strange existence under one roof. His mother made sure the house was run superior to anyone else's, in her opinion. The social events they hosted were among the finest among the ton. They enjoyed the finest of what life had, but Trent wondered if they were truly happy. He could remember when he was a child how inseparable and in love they were. Now they tolerated each other, and if there was any affection between them, it was kept behind closed doors.

He and Eugenie would never go down that road. He couldn't imagine not waking up to his beautiful bride. Certainly, there would be times she would take to her own chambers, but not now. It seemed to him even her parents' marriage was similar to his own parents'. Perhaps that was part of the reason the two couples got along so well.

"I hate to say it," Eugenie said as they watched the two carriages disappear down the long tree lined drive, "but I thought they would never leave. Or worse yet, our mothers would concoct some excuse to spend the night."

"That would have been a nightmare I can live without. Not that I don't love my mother; I do. I just prefer she live her life now and let me live mine."

Eugenie laughed at the thought. "They wore me out."

"How's that? My mother wasn't that bad, was she?"

"She and my mother had to put their approval on the house, gave me endless tips on running the household. And you?"

"More business from our fathers. How powerful our two families are now because of our marriage. What business deals they wished to jointly pursue, such as allowing the railroad access to build on our estates." he replied.

"But wouldn't that be noisy?"

He shook his head. "No, the access they're being given is at the far end of our estates."

"They could have done it without our being married, couldn't they?"

"Perhaps. This gives them prestige, makes both our

families more powerful," he replied. "It's complicated and involves more than just railway access."

He led her into the house and up the stairs. She paused, then walked toward the drawing room in which they'd just been entertaining. "I really think I could use a brandy, if you don't mind."

"That bad?"

She smiled. God, he loved it when she smiled. She was so self-assured and confident in herself. "You have no idea. I think they both thought our postponing our wedding trip was for the best, but your mother assured me it would probably not happen even then."

"Why's that?" he asked. He poured them both a brandy and handed his wife one of the snifters.

"Because I'll be with child by then, and traveling anywhere will have to be forsaken."

He felt the sides of his mouth pull up. "That sounds like my mother."

"Do you want to hear the best part?"

"Amuse me."

She smiled again like she was keeping some naughty secret. "If you're like your father, you'll have me with child, if I'm not already."

"She didn't."

"Oh, I can assure you she did."

"I apologize for her behavior, sweet."

Eugenie shook her head. "Don't. My mother was in the thick of it all with her. They're both forces to be reckoned with. They're double trouble when they're together."

He took a long swallow. "I think I understand now."

"Hopefully, this visit has satisfied any questions or curiosity on our mothers' part."

"For a while I'm sure. Don't forget their joint summer house party."

Eugenie groaned and shook her head. "I completely forgot."

"I'm trying to figure a way we can be away when they hold it. Otherwise, our lives will be put on hold and we'll be taken hostage by our mothers."

Trent sat down next to her. "There is a ship that our fathers and I are having built in Southampton. They put me in charge of the project. We could travel there so I may see firsthand how it's progressing. On the way back, we could stop in Bath, or better yet, we'll be near the Isle of Wight. Perhaps we could spend a few days there."

"Oh, yes, let's!"

He took a sip of brandy. "I think it would be a perfect holiday, and if we plan it well, we would be away for most of our parents' house party."

"It would. I can't wait to see this ship you're having built. What do you plan to use it for?"

"Hauling goods between here and America mainly. This ship is a steam ship, so it'll be quicker."

"I didn't think there were a lot of ocean-going steam vessels," she said.

"You're right. They're mostly regulated to rivers and lakes, but there have been several successful ocean faring ships. This one will be different. It will have sails in case the crew encounter a problem with the engines."

"Whose idea was that?"

"Mine. I've been quite involved with its development and convincing our fathers that this was the future of shipping."

"You have a great many interests."

"I do," he agreed. He picked up his snifter and drained the contents. "We could also stop by and see how training is progressing on a mare I bought on our way back."

"A racer?"

160

He nodded. "Yes. She has much potential, so I decided she needed a proper racing trainer."

"I'm intrigued," she said, holding out her empty glass to him. "One more, and then we'll retire to our chambers."

He smiled and took the snifter. "Is my wife indulging herself?"

The answer came quickly. "Your wife has had a particularly trying day."

He set the glass down on the table next to him. With his fingers, he traced the outline of her jaw and tipped her face up. "Come, I keep spirits in my sitting room. We can continue our discussion there." He leaned down and kissed her lightly on the lips.

"That sounds divine. I can't wait to take this blasted corset and shoes off."

Trent smiled at the thought and stood, extending his hand to her. "Come. I can help you with that."

"My maid waits. I'll have her loosen my corset and send her off for the night. If that meets with your approval, my lord."

He helped her to her feet and nodded. "It most certainly does, wife."

"Lead the way."

He tucked her hand in the crook of his arm and walked out of the drawing room. They headed up the stairs and to Trent's room. In the short time they'd been married, his bed seemed to be the one they used. It was old, ornately carved, and large. It was positioned so that if there were ever a need for the marquess to be abed late in the day, he could look out the windows and gaze upon the rolling meadows.

Trent watched her disappear behind the door that joined the two bedchambers. He strode over to a sideboard in the sitting room and poured two brandies. His valet had already been here, closing the heavy drapes, turning back the bed, and making sure the fire warmed the room efficiently. Even in summer, the evenings could be cool.

Removing his cravat, he left it on the sideboard, and taking the two brandy snifters walked over to a leather chair. He sat down and removed his boots, followed by his jacket, and waited on Eugenie, who didn't take long to reappear.

She had taken her hair down, and it softly framed her face in the firelight. He held out a snifter of brandy, which she accepted. She was barefoot as well, and Trent noted she wore no stockings. Too bad because he liked removing them from her long, sensual legs.

Eugenie walked over to the fireplace and turned toward him. "When will we leave for Southampton?"

"Three days too soon?"

"Not at all," she replied, taking a sip of brandy.

"We could leave day after tomorrow, but I know you need time to pack, and I need to write to the shipbuilder in Southampton to let him know I plan on coming to visit."

"My maid is quite efficient and can have me packed quickly if the need arises."

They passed the next few minutes in perfect silence. Trent knew he had to ask. He'd found her shawl on the floor near the door of the drawing room leading to the terrace. Had she been listening in, and if she had, what had she heard?

"Did you misplace your shawl this afternoon?" He took a drink and watched her ponder her answer.

"Yes. I looked all over for it. I assumed I left it in one of the rooms I took our mothers to when I was giving them a tour of the house. Where was it?"

"In the drawing room, near the French doors," he muttered. "Were you eavesdropping?"

He watched her closely to see how her mannerisms might change. If they did.

"I was curious to see what you three were talking about, yes. I wouldn't really call that eavesdropping. Curious is what I'd call it."

"That's perfectly fine, but understand this; it isn't easy trying to live up to the expectations that have been placed on me. Our fathers wish our families to be set for generations to come."

"But hadn't they been?"

"Yes, but now, having our family intertwined gives them more of a sense of power. That's not me, and I find myself conflicted by some of their demands."

"Demands?"

He stopped for a moment to choose his words carefully. "They want me, my father in particular, to be part of some business dealings they have. I feel conflicted because even though I'll work with them, I still want to manage my own interests," he replied, then cocked his head in her direction. "Does that make any sense, or have I confused you more?"

She graced him with a smile and walked back over to him. She placed her brandy snifter on a nearby table and took both his hands. "Yes, I can understand why you're conflicted. You've been educated and trained all your life to become duke, and until your father passes, you'd like to engage in your own interests. Am I right?"

"Yes. That's exactly how I'm feeling. I was never allowed to have any outside interests until I went off to university. Then once I settled in with my responsibilities as marquess, I began to branch out."

She sat down on his lap and put her arms around his neck. "You ought to have been raised in my shoes. Being schooled in everything that would make me a perfect duchess one day. Your duchess. I know our parents wanted this, and I know you were pressured, but

I'm thankful we get along with or without any help from anyone else. We have a deep and binding love, Trent."

"Yes, we do. I ache for you when you're not near. You're constantly in my thoughts, from the time I awaken until I fall asleep at night. I love you, Eugenie, with all my heart."

"And I love you, always and forever."

CHAPTER 16

*E*ugenie marveled at the elegance of Tatum House. It was one of the three properties her husband had received upon finishing Cambridge. Trent's grandfather had designed the house himself of an Italian Renaissance palazzo, complete with two belvedere towers. It sat on a seaside plot of land, overlooking the channel. Below the well-maintained gardens was a private beach.

"Does this meet with your approval?" Trent asked. He walked up behind her and wrapped his arms around her as they gazed out at the water together.

"Yes, much better than the hotel in Southampton, don't you think?"

"The two cannot be compared," he rumbled.

"Did this come with your title?"

"It did. My grandfather gifted it to my father. My mother's never been fond of the house. We rarely ever came here, so he passed it to me."

"Well, I hope you never pass it on to our son. I think I should like spending time here."

"I know if you like it, I shall as well," he said. "Would you like me to show you the house, or would you like to walk down to the beach? The tide is out, so now would be a perfect time."

She turned and smiled up at him as he loosened his grip on her. "Yes, let's. Afterwards I'll see about having lunch served outdoors."

"Perfect. I am famished. Breakfast is a distant memory."

"Would you rather not go to the beach right now?"

"No, let's go walk in the sand. As I said, the tide is coming in, and we won't be able to later."

They continued on through the well-maintained gardens. Continuing through a white painted gate, Eugenie walked alongside her husband. Finally, she stopped to take off her boots, leaving them on top of a large boulder that sat next to the pathway.

"Come," she said, grabbing Trent's hand. "Take your boots off. Let's put our feet in the water and walk."

"You go on ahead. I'll meet up with you in a few minutes," he replied.

She knew she'd won him over and cracked her husband's rock-solid facade. She loved the idea that he felt comfortable enough with her that he was willing to drop all properness and enjoy himself with her. Most men, husbands of friends, even her own father hid behind a door of being untouchable, never laughing, rarely smiling. It gave her heart joy to see him so relaxed.

She came up on the soft sand and water gently lapping up on the shore. The water was cold to the touch, but standing at the edge, the water surrounding her ankles, Eugenie held her skirts up, giggling as she waited on her husband.

Trent neared her, taking her hand. They began to walk down the beach.

"I can see us coming here quite often. It'll be the perfect spot for family holidays," she said.

"Planning ahead, are you?"

"Of course. Families don't spend enough time together."

He smiled. "I would have to agree with you and hope we don't end up allowing others to raise our children."

"That's why somewhere like this is perfect. The children can still have their nannies or governesses come along, but here children can be free. Free to spend more time with us."

"I would think you plan on spending a lot more time with our children than our own mothers did."

She smiled, tucking her hand in his forearm. "I do, but first I must be with child."

Trent patted her hand. "Perhaps we can work on that later this afternoon. After lunch?"

"Oh, I think we should, my lord."

She stopped suddenly, looking down the beach towards their closest neighbor. The property was owned by a shipping magnet, who brought his family to Wight for the summers. She pointed to a fixture high in the sand.

"Is that one of those bathing machines?"

"Yes. Haven't you seen one before?"

"From afar."

"Perhaps we can impose on our neighbors so you may have a look."

"I would like that, but I don't think we should bother our neighbors."

They walked along in silence for a moment, the only sound the water lapping up and the gulls screeching.

"They are available for rent in the village. Maybe we could look at one there."

"Yes, perhaps we could take a drive through the village and beyond. I'd love to see more of the island," she said. She removed herself from Trent's arm, racing ahead. She stopped, leaned over and began splashing water on him as he neared.

She laughed and began running back toward the gardens, Trent on her heels, but keeping enough of a distance to let her think she was quicker than he was. He caught her and hauled her into his arms, leaned down, and kissed her.

"I think lunch is in order, my lord."

"It's what I crave after our meal that I want."

She sat against the boulder and put her boots back on, watching as Trent did the same. "Well, perhaps you can show me the house before we retire to our chamber."

"I should like that very much," he replied. "If I remember correctly, there is an unused bedchamber on the top floor. I'm not sure why it's there, but there's a rumor it was a private meeting place for my parents when they first married. Somewhere they could be alone without interruption from staff. Only the butler knew of the room's existence, and he died years ago."

"Sounds intriguing."

Walking into the house, Eugenie rang for the butler to inquire on lunch and where she wanted it served. She had taken to her new position as marchioness flawlessly. She had a way with people. Everyone adored her. Trent knew when it came time, she would make a wonderful duchess.

THEY TOOK their meal on the terrace, which overlooked the gardens and water. Various smoked meats, cheese, fruit, and fresh bread made up their meal. Lemonade was also served, and she hid a smile, knowing her husband wasn't overly fond of the beverage. He drank it without a word.

"You were satisfied with how your ship is progressing?" she asked, picking up a fresh plump strawberry.

"Yes, other than the fact it's behind schedule. But that's through no fault of the builder. Key parts were delayed, but I'm confident the delivery schedule will be met."

"Wouldn't it be better to have the ship behind and building progress correctly than it be put together in a rush?"

He tore off a piece of bread and chewed thoughtfully. "Yes, of course. The ship will be at sea under a variety of weather conditions. It has to be built without a flaw, especially this one, given the steam engines."

"I shall look forward to seeing it once it's finished."

Trent took an apple and cut it into slices. "Have you ever thought about perhaps going somewhere on a ship? America? I've always wanted to go to New York City or Boston."

"I've always wanted to visit faraway lands. You know that."

He smiled. "Yes, I remember."

"Maybe your business ventures will take you to New York or Boston, and someday we could make the voyage."

"I expect they will," he replied. "Enough about business."

"We need to finish quickly. It looks as though a storm is headed our way."

"Part of the enjoyment of being on the coast. You can watch the storms as they roll in."

"Come, if you are finished, we can take our dessert inside and watch without getting wet."

They hurried inside to the drawing room while the footmen scurried to take away the dishes and food before the first drops of rain hit the ground. Trent sat in a chair while Eugenie cut him a slice of chocolate cake the cook had made. It was one of her husband's favorites and she wondered if the cook knew that and had it baked just for today.

She cut herself a small slice as well and walked across the room to join her husband. She handed him the plate and fork and sat down next to him. The sky had darkened as the first drops of rain were beginning to fall.

Eugenie sat down and took a bite of cake while watching the weather unfold just outside the open French doors. "I've always thought the way the weather changes on the coast is simply amazing, how the sea air pushes a change of weather onto land."

"Yes, the force of storms has always been of keen interest to me. Remember when we rode across our family estates as children?"

She nodded, taking a bite of cake. She appeared to be delighting in every bite of the dessert. "How could I forget? We had some rather special times."

Thunder rattled the windows as the storm intensified. "We did, and now we'll make our own special memories."

"Goodness, I think we ought to shut that door before the rain pours in."

He reached across and rubbed her cheek with his finger. "Come, I promised to take you exploring."

She followed him out of the drawing room and up another flight of steps leading to the bed chambers and other private family rooms. The floor above was primarily used for storage, though he'd spoken of somewhere special. She followed quietly as he led her down a narrow hall to a locked door. He removed a key from one of his jacket pockets and opened the door.

Trent followed her in, and he closed the door, locking it behind him. He watched her as she curiously walked around the room, taking in all the furnishings and the room. There, against the far wall, was a bed which he'd made sure was made and waiting. Sneaking away from Eugenie to gather sheets and other linens hadn't been easy as he was unfamiliar with where the housekeeper kept such things. He finally found them and quickly had come and readied the room.

"I thought no one knew of the room's existence?"

He smiled. "No one does. I retrieved the linens while you were busy elsewhere, and cleaned the room as best I could. As I told you, since the old butler died, I doubt anyone has knowledge of this room or its use."

"I think I should like to find somewhere in our country estate as well. I like having somewhere away from prying eyes."

"Your wish is my command," he replied. He closed the space between them and began to unbutton her dress with his expert fingers. The dress puddled on the floor at her feet. She stepped out of it to allow him to unlace her corset. He nuzzled her neck as he did. "You are so exquisite, my love."

Without a word, she lifted a leg onto the bed. "Would you care to take my stockings off after I remove my boots, my lord?"

"No, I think I should like you with your stockings on for now."

She stood and removed her undergarments, standing completely naked in front of Trent. Except for her white stockings with pink ribbons. If his cock hadn't been hard before, it was now. Eugenie crawled up onto the bed on her hands and knees, making sure Trent got an eyeful, teasing him.

He began to quickly remove his clothes, eager to devour her. She was spread out against the pillows, her legs spread wide open for him. Her eyes were heavy from desire, beckoning him without words.

Quickly, he covered her body with his, spreading

feather kisses along her face, to her ears, and down her graceful, long neck. She moaned in delight as he went lower. He lifted one breast in his hand and suckled her, nipping at the hardened tip before moving on to the other. She was such a magnificent creature. He couldn't believe he'd been so lucky. Eugenie was willing and eager to learn from him, and he had much to teach her.

The storm raged around them, shaking the windows as they became lost in each other.

TRENT AWOKE, Eugenie nestled in his arms. The storm still raged outside. Not unusual for this time of year or for the coast. They had snuck away, away from prying servants and lost themselves in each other.

It was nearly impossible to tell the time with the dark clouds. Slowly, he began to wake his bride, smothering her with kisses. She burrowed her face against his chest.

"Come, love. I can't be sure how long we've been here or what time it is, but we need to dress. We can return another day."

"Do we have to?" she asked softly.

He kissed the top of her head, his hands stroking her hair. "I'm afraid so."

"Very well, if we must."

"Don't despair. We'll sneak away again."

She sighed. "I suppose you have correspondence and things to take care of?"

"It wouldn't hurt if I kept ahead of it."

"Yes, I'm sure," she replied, irritation in her voice. "I suppose I can walk through the house and see where everything is."

"I thought tomorrow we could take a carriage tour of the island."

"Oh, yes! I'd love that, Trent. I understand the Queen has her summer home here as well."

"I'm not sure I'd call it a summer home as she visits at all times of the year."

"Still, I would love to see it if it's visible."

"There are plenty of other notable homes to see if it is not."

She pushed away from him and sat up. He watched her push her hair out of her face before she stood up. "You know what else I'd like to try while we're here?"

"What's that?" he asked softly.

"I think I should like to try one of those bathing machines."

He grinned. "Really?"

"Yes, really, though I don't have a bathing costume."

"Perhaps you might find one in the village."

She began to button her chemise. Her drawers still lay on the floor where he'd discarded them earlier.

"If I don't, I suppose my modiste could make one when we return to London."

"Which I was planning on doing when we leave here. Just for a couple of days. Then we'll go back to the country."

"Can we come back here before summer's over?"

"Of course we can, love."

Dressed, they quietly left their sanctuary on the top floor. Trent led them back to his bedchamber before kissing her and leaving her. "I won't be long; I promise."

"I think I'm going to bathe and change clothes before I go back downstairs. Hopefully, the storm might pass soon," she said, glancing at a clock that sat on the mantle. "It's later than I thought. Go. I'll see to tea when I finish here."

"Very well." He kissed her swollen lips before turning and leaving the room. He knew if he stayed, they'd be back in bed since Trent had no self-control when it came to his delectable wife.

Eugenie turned to find the bathing chamber in the marchioness's suite. Her lady's maid had readied everything for her. She began to fill the tub with hot water as she undressed, thinking about the time she and Trent had shared.

At the rate they made love, it would surely be no time before a child was conceived, if it hadn't been already. She placed her hand softly on her belly and smiled.

As she began to lower herself into the steaming water, her maid appeared. Eugenie grabbed the soap and cloth as the woman picked up her clothes, humming as she did.

"I think I should like to wear the lavender dress," she said as she soaped up the cloth.

"I have it ready, my lady. I'll lay it out on the bed."

"Thank you. Also, if the weather is nice tomorrow, Lord Trent intends to take us on a carriage ride through the island, and I'll need something for it."

"Your pale yellow would look splendid I think," she replied.

"Yes. That will work nicely."

"I'll take it downstairs to press now, my lady. Unless you need anything else?"

"No, go ahead and take it. By the time you return, I'll be ready for your assistance."

"Yes, my lady."

The maid turned with her handful of clothing and disappeared into the closets. Eugenie sighed and sat back in the tub to enjoy her bath. She closed her eyes for a few minutes and relaxed. Upon opening her eyes, she noted the sun was coming back out. The window in the bathing chamber was filled with warm sunlight.

She submerged herself beneath the water in order

to wash her hair. Usually, her maid helped her with this, but today she was thankful to have some time alone. When she finished, she rinsed her hair beneath the water.

An hour later she was finished, looking nothing like the disheveled, love struck young woman of an hour ago. She looked one final time in the mirror before quitting the room and heading downstairs.

Like she had at Trent Estate, she wanted to find the kitchens and introduce herself to the cook and see how far out the woman might have menus planned.

She walked down the stairs to the next level. Quite by accident, she found Trent's study, only because he'd left the door partially open. She stood silently in front of it before knocking and entering the dark paneled room.

Trent was immersed in papers spread out in front of him. At first, he didn't notice when she entered. Not until she stood at the opposite side of the large oak desk.

"Must be terribly important," she whispered.

His head jerked up. He smiled when he realized who it was who'd entered. "I didn't hear you come in. Please, sit." He glanced down at the papers. "Going over a contract I brought with me."

"I won't keep you from your work."

He reached out across the desk and took her hand. "I promise I won't be much longer."

"While you're working, I'm going to the kitchen and introduce myself to the cook. I'll have tea sent to the drawing room."

He smiled and looked down at his work. "I'll be ready for a break."

She turned and left his study, shutting the door behind her. A footman passed her. She stopped him and asked him if she was going down the right hall towards the kitchens. When Eugenie entered, she found the kitchen in a disarray. The woman she took to be the cook, as well as the housekeeper she recognized from when they'd first arrived were fussing over the stove.

As Eugenie neared, she could hear something being said about the stove not staying lit. The housekeeper noticed her first and introduced the cook as well as a couple of other kitchen maids.

"I'm afraid you've come at a bad time, my lady."

"What is the problem with the stove?" Eugenie asked.

"It won't stay lit," the cook moaned.

"It looks rather old. Has anyone approached the marquess or his estate manager about possibly replacing it?"

The cook shook her head. "Mr. Patten says to make do, but if I can't get it lit, I'm afraid I won't be able to have dinner prepared."

"I'll speak with the Marquess myself," Eugenie said. She turned to a footman who was polishing silver on another table. "In fact, ask my husband if he would come here. Explain the situation, and tell him I need him to help."

The young man nodded and left the room. After he left, Eugenie moved closer to get an even better look. The stove certainly did need updating, but that wouldn't help if the cook had nothing to prepare dinner.

"If the stove can't be lit, could you not possibly prepare a chicken on the hearth?"

The woman nodded. "Yes, of course. That would solve tonight's meal. I'll get on it."

"Let's wait and see if the Marquess has any ideas. He's quite good at fixing things. Maybe he can get it working until a replacement can be delivered."

A few minutes later Trent strode into the room. Eugenie was afraid he might be annoyed by being disturbed, but instead he arched a brow when he looked at the old stove. "This thing is probably older than my father. Let me see what I can do."

"Thank you, my lord," the cook said.

"It does need replacing. Tomorrow I want you and Mr. Patten to go to the village. If you don't find what you want, order it. We'll make do until it's delivered, and I want you to order the best stove. No need not having the most up to date."

Cook bobbed her head and gazed at him with wide eyes. Trent rolled up his sleeves and began to tinker with the old iron beast. It took him a while, but soon he had the stove where it would keep a fire.

Satisfied, he stood and smiled. "Hopefully, if you keep it going tonight, it'll stay lit through the night."

"Thank you, my lord," Cook said, beaming.

"It's not much of a fix, but I hope we can keep it going until a new one can be delivered."

Eugenie looked at him with fondness. The way he took care of his staff and household was one of the many virtues she loved about Trent. He could have easily had Cook make do with the failing stove. Instead, he was sending her to the village to pick one out. This wasn't their primary residence, but Trent believed they should all be in perfect working order.

He stopped next to her as he was leaving the kitchen. "I'm going to clean up. Why don't we have tea in the drawing room?"

"I'll see to it and meet you there."

With the disaster averted in the kitchen, Eugenie went about having tea sent to the drawing room. She thanked everyone and found her way there. She loved the pale blue color, complimented by various shades of yellow. The furniture was covered in upholstery in similar shades. It made the room warm and appealing.

The storm had let up, and sun now replaced the black sky. It was late afternoon, she noted from the clock and the angle of the sun in the sky. She opened the doors while waiting on tea and her husband to arrive. The storm had cooled things down, but she had hopes that she and Trent might enjoy a glass of wine before dinner on the terrace.

Eugenie turned, hearing a noise behind her. A footman, along with the butler, were setting a large tray on a side table. She noted a tea service and two plates. One had small sandwiches, while the other contained decadent small cakes.

Trent, never one to miss food, especially when he was hungry, strode into the room. She neared as he greeted her with a kiss.

"Come, let me pour you a cup."

"Everything looks remarkable," he replied as he picked up a plate and began to help himself to sandwiches and cakes.

"Thank you for solving the stove dilemma. I think you should have a meeting with your estate manager, housekeeper, and cook and make sure there isn't anything else needing replacement."

"You're right of course," he replied, biting into a roast beef sandwich. "Aren't you going to have anything to eat?"

Her stomach was in distress, but it was probably because of the busy day. She hadn't eaten since before they'd arrived, which was not usual. She picked up a piece of shortbread to nibble on, but even it didn't hold much appeal.

Sipping her tea, she listened to Trent give her more facts about the island, then move on to their return back to Gloucestershire. One thing about her husband, he was organized and kept a well-maintained schedule.

CHAPTER 17

*E*ugenie awoke at dawn the following morning. The heavy draperies had already been opened, and the faint pinkish-gray light of dawn was brightening the sky. She lay there gazing over where Trent had slept. He was an early riser and obviously had work to attend to. He took his duties seriously, better than most men of his wealth and position. Most of them delegated such matters to estate managers and solicitors, only taking their word on how the properties and other interests fared.

A wave of nausea overtook her as she sat up. She steadied herself, waiting for it to subside, but another round came. She had no time to be sick, especially not while they were on holiday in such a lovely spot as the Isle of Wight.

She called out to Mona, her lady's maid, who immediately appeared out of nowhere.

"See that a tray of tea and toast is brought. I believe I'll catch up on some correspondence while the marquess is working."

"Yes, my lady. Is that all?" Mona asked as she bobbed and turned to leave.

"That's all for now."

Another wave of nausea hit her as her maid left the room. Eugenie walked over to the windows and looked out as she pulled her robe on, hoping any distraction might make it go away. Certainly, she couldn't be ill; to her knowledge, they hadn't been around anyone who might have been ill.

Then it hit her; women who were with child were often sick in the morning. It certainly was a possibility. She and Trent had done nothing to prevent a pregnancy; in fact, they'd discussed on numerous occasions starting a family of their own.

Still, she would keep it under wraps until she was sure. If her maid mentioned anything, she would swear her to secrecy until she could confirm her suspicions and tell Trent the wonderful news.

She sat down at a desk that sat before the windows. It overlooked the gardens and sea. A peaceful, tranquil view. She had received a letter from Lady Alice Hamilton, a childhood friend who'd married the Earl of Hamilton. She and Lady Hamilton had spent two seasons together before Alice was betrothed to the earl.

Eugenie recalled how envious she'd been at the time when her friend had married for love and not family obligation. Fortunately, it had worked out that way for her and Trent. Others were not as fortunate. Her childhood friend Lady Margaret Horn, for example. Her father, a viscount, had married her off to a mere baron just to be rid of her. The baron was at least ten years her senior, and the man regarded her as his property, nothing more. So much so, the baron would not allow her to partake in teas or other social events when everyone was in London, keeping her isolated.

Her thoughts were interrupted by Mona carrying a tray with a pot of tea and plate of toast. Eugenie motioned her to place it on a table alongside the desk. She put her pen down and walked over to the tray to fix herself a cup of tea.

She resumed her writing, stopping only to take a bit of toast or sip of tea. She had so much to tell Alice that it made her long for the days when they were carefree girls who could visit each other for hours to gossip and tell secrets. Now society dictated her social life.

Eugenie told her friend of hers and Trent's visit to Southampton where he had a ship being built, and about their holiday at the marquess's other estate on the Isle of Wight. Though she was so far enjoying her stay, her mind always wandered back to the country. She could ride there for countless hours and still not cover all the grounds.

She tried to explain the house and its magnificent gardens leading down to the sea, but she did not tell Alice what she suspected. She would tell no one until she was sure.

Hearing her maid making up the bed, she called out to her.

"Mona, I believe I'll dress now. The marquess and I will be going on a carriage ride today, so I believe the yellow dress will do nicely."

"Yes, my lady. I'll get everything ready."

Eugenie folded the letter and readied it. She dressed quickly. It was too lovely a day to be inside, and there was much to see and do. Her stomach had subsided and returned to normal, and she prayed it wouldn't betray her later.

She found Trent in his study, poring over a pile of papers, completely lost in his work. If he heard her enter, he didn't acknowledge her.

"Good morning," she said after watching him work for a couple of minutes.

He grunted something, what she couldn't tell.

Whatever it was, perhaps she wasn't supposed to make sense of it.

"Trent?"

He finally pulled his eyes from the stack of papers. "Yes?"

"Are you not going to eat this morning?"

He shook his head. "Maybe later. There are some serious discrepancies I have to try and resolve."

"Would you like me to bring you something, perhaps some coffee or tea?" She knew he preferred coffee in the morning.

"I said I wasn't hungry, Eugenie. Now, please, I need to get this done," he bit out.

"Very well. I'll leave you," she replied in disbelief of his dismissal of her. "I take it you have no interest in going to the village to purchase a new stove?"

"No, that is why I'm sending Cook and Mr. Patten. Go, handle it yourself. Get whatever is top of the line."

She was being dismissed. He'd never been so abrupt with her. His tone stung and hurt her feelings, which never had happened before. Watching him work as though she didn't exist, she turned and left the room, closing the door behind her. She would just have to make the best of the day. She'd go into the village and purchase a stove, then spend some time looking at the various shops. If he was still deep into his paper work when she finished, she would take herself on a tour of the island.

She rode into the village and found the shop owner waiting on her. Someone, either Trent or the estate manager, had alerted the man to the fact that the marchioness would be coming to choose a stove. As neither the cook nor the estate manager were available, Eugenie went alone, accompanied only by her maid.

Eugenie stood and listened as the shop keeper went over the two best stoves he had to offer. It seemed to her that the man was trying to convince her the one he wished to sell her was better than the one he wasn't showing her.

She thanked the man, then moved on to the next one, which was slightly more expensive but had new features that would last for many generations. He hesitated but explained how it worked and its advantages. He appeared flustered to have a woman in his shop determined to make such a large purchase.

In the end, she made her choice and went with the better, more expensive stove. The shop owner hesitated but nodded and assured her the new one would be delivered as soon as it could be arranged with her cook. Installation would take several hours and would require the old one to be dismantled and removed before installation could begin.

Satisfied with her purchase, Eugenie thanked the man. She decided while she was there to purchase a few items she needed. A sketch pad and pencils since her maid had failed to bring her supplies with them, and Eugenie was eager to sketch the gardens and the view of the sea.

She gathered her purchases and handed them to a footman waiting by the carriage. The carriage was still in front of the shop where she'd purchased the stove. Looking closer, she could see that Trent's estate manager and the shop owner were in a deep discussion. It struck her as odd since the man couldn't take the time to go with her to make the purchase.

Arriving home, she quickly went in search of Trent. He was still going over a pile of papers, but this time he was furiously writing.

"I just thought I'd check on you," she said from the doorway.

He put the pen down and rose from his chair. He

walked toward her. "Did you find a stove to your liking?"

"I would have preferred Cook could have accompanied me, but I think she'll be pleased with what I chose."

"Good," he replied, taking her hand. "I apologize for earlier. I found some irregularities, and I'm not only trying to rectify them, I'm trying to figure out where they came from and by whom."

"That sounds quite ominous. I'll understand if we must postpone our carriage ride. I can sketch instead."

He kissed her cheek. "How about we go for our ride later this afternoon. If I haven't finished, I'll put it aside, I promise."

"I'm holding you to that, my lord."

"I'm sure you will." He was a tall man, so Eugenie stood on tip toes and kissed him on the cheek. "I'll leave you to your papers. Would you care for something to eat while you work?"

"Some tea and perhaps scones might do the trick."

Eugenie walked to the kitchen to ask that a tray be sent to Trent's study. When she went through the door, the first thing she noticed was workmen taking out the old stove. She found the cook outside looking at the brand-new shiny stove that had been taken off the wagon. It wasn't the one she'd ordered.

"This is not the stove I ordered, and it wasn't supposed to be delivered until tomorrow," Eugenie said in disbelief.

No one said anything for a moment. Cook, however, moved away and nodded. "I'll fix his lordship some tea. I made scones earlier and will send him a plate."

"Thank you."

She glanced over at the estate manager, who was looking rather smug. She wanted to say something. She should tell Trent about it first, but she was the marchioness, and she ran the house, not the estate manager and not the housekeeper.

"Explain yourself, sir. Why wasn't the stove I chose delivered, and why is it being delivered today and not tomorrow?"

"The one you chose was too frivolous. This one will do just fine. When I inquired, the shopkeeper saw he had a way to deliver it today."

"Send it back. I want the one I ordered."

"Don't worry yourself about such things, my lady. The matter is settled."

Eugenie turned to leave. "The matter is not settled, nor do I want this stove. I'll speak with the marquess. He'll settle the matter once and for all."

"That's your choice, my lady. I am certain, though, he'll agree with me."

She turned to the workmen. "Stop what you're doing. I'll bring the marquess to settle the matter."

She marched out of the kitchen and quickly found Trent's office once again. He had two ledgers open this time. For a brief second, she wondered what he'd found, but the situation in the kitchen needed immediate attention.

"Trent, I'm sorry to bother you, but there's a matter that's developed in the kitchen, and I need your help."

He looked up from the books and sat back in his chair. "Eugenie, you're going to have to learn to take care of any and all household matters. I can't always be there to fix things for you."

"I understand, but this particular situation is going to require your assistance."

She stood in front of him and quickly explained what was going on in the kitchen, how her stove choice had been changed, and how she was being treated by the estate manager.

Trent stood up and came around the desk. "I'm

sorry, my love. Of course your choices and directives should be respected. Come, I'll go to the kitchen with you and clear the matter up. Perhaps it's simply a misunderstanding."

"Thank you. I know this isn't our primary residence, but I still expect to be respected as mistress of this house."

"I don't care if we are only in residence once a year. You are mistress of the house and will be treated as such."

They returned to the kitchen to find the old stove had been completely removed from the kitchen. When everyone saw the marquess, their attitudes changed immediately.

"I thought the marchioness told you to stop until I returned with her," Trent said, his attention focused squarely on his estate manager.

"My apologies, my lord. I thought it best to finish removing the old one."

"What were you going to replace it with? The marchioness informs me that the one sitting outside on the wagon is not the one she ordered."

"A stove's a stove, isn't it, my lord?"

"Not if it isn't the one my wife ordered. I suggest you return the one you have sitting on the wagon and return with the correct stove."

"Yes, my lord, though I'm not sure he'll have that one available today."

"And I'm sure you'll see that it happens. Whatever it takes," Trent replied. "I would also like to clear up a matter while I am here. The marchioness is lady of the house, and thereby in charge of its running. We might only visit a few times a year, but it is still my house, and therefore my wife's. If she asks something, you are to do so without question."

A murmur of voices could be heard all in agreement. Eugenie followed her husband back to his study. He shut the door and placed his hands on either side of her face. "You were right to come get me. I trust I got my point across, and you won't have any further problems."

"I have a feeling I won't be having any more problems. Thank you."

"Never be afraid to come to me, no matter how small the matter might seem. A lot of men are unused to a woman having the ability to make decisions for herself."

"Thank goodness you aren't one of those."

He kissed her on the lips. "I also think it's time for me to put this aside. I need a distraction before I return to all these papers."

"What sort of distraction, my lord?"

"How about we take that carriage ride. We could go through the village and perhaps pick up a basket for lunch. Some wine, and have a picnic somewhere."

"I would love that, Trent. You're sure you can spare the time?" Her gaze drew over his ledgers and papers spread out on his desk.

"Yes, I'm quite sure."

"Then let's go."

Before he let her go, Trent kissed her again. "I apologize if I was gruff earlier."

She smiled demurely. "You don't have to explain yourself. I know you have a lot going on."

"Thank you for understanding. Now, I'll go see to the carriage," he said.

She nodded. "I'll go gather my shawl, and I'll meet you in the grand hall."

He let her go, watching her hips sway as she walked to the door. How had he gotten so lucky? To have a wife who was smart, educated, and not shy to speak her mind was more than he could have asked for. Now he just had to learn how to separate the amount of time he spent in his study and join his wife on more pleasant matters such as going for a drive.

What displeased him was staff not treating his wife, the marchioness, with the respect her title and position deserved. She should be able to run the household without problems and without being questioned. He understood it might take time; he just wasn't sure how long.

He found himself questioning the purchase of the new stove. Trent was already looking into some of the household accounts, finding discrepancies. It appeared at first glance that something was indeed amiss. Finding it would take some time and patience on his part, and if there were something going on, he would find it. He had other, more pressing matters, but this didn't need to get out of hand, which was why he was determined to scour the household accounts until he was satisfied.

COOK SENT them off with a basket of cheese, fresh bread, some smoked meats, and apples, along with a bottle of wine. Trent made sure he thanked the woman, especially since her kitchen was in disarray with the stove installation. It ended up saving them from having to ride through the village to procure a basket. Trent had somewhere in the opposite direction in mind for their lunch.

Trent's original destination for this outing was further out than they had time for today. They'd gotten a late start due to the kitchen matter. There was a bluff a couple of miles toward the east side of the island. It was uninhabited, and though it didn't have access to the beach below, there was a small grove of windblown trees that would protect them from the wind. He'd found it when riding on his first visit. On a good day, one could see the mainland of England. As clear as it was today, they might be as lucky.

The bay gelding slowed as Trent brought the gig to a stop. Eugenie took in her surroundings as she waited for him to help her down.

"Where exactly are we?" she asked as he lifted her down from the gig.

"At the easternmost point of the isle. I'm surprised no one has bought up the land and built a house. The view can be spectacular from here."

"How's that?"

He gazed down at her and watched her tongue flick over her lips. "You can not only see to the coast, on a good day, you can see further up the coast. I'm hoping we have such a day."

"It's awfully windblown here. I doubt much would grow. At least we have the gardens."

"Growing a garden here would take years to cultivate," he replied. Trent grabbed the basket from the back of the gig, handing Eugenie a lightweight blanket for them to sit on.

They walked through the small grove of trees. On the other side, on the bluff, was a small patch of grass, which looked out of place. Trent chose a spot near some large bushes that would help shield them from the winds. Today wasn't as bad as the last time he'd visited this spot, but he wanted her to enjoy their time.

"This is very nice, Trent," she said. She spread the blanket with his help, and he placed the basket on one side.

"It's the highest bluff on this side of the isle," he said. "Perhaps next time we can get an earlier start and go further around the isle."

"I would like that. Maybe next time we could ride?"

"Yes, that would make for a wonderful day. There's another village a few miles off if you continue to follow the road. Not close, but it would be somewhere we could perhaps have lunch."

"Let's plan to do it, and soon."

He arched a brow. "We have time, my love. I foresee us being her for at least a fortnight."

"Then will we return to London or the country?"

"I thought we'd skip London. If I need my solicitors, they can come to the country. It's not all that far."

"Good, because London in the summer is not so pleasant."

He barked out a laugh. "No, it isn't. It can be quite dreadful some months."

She opened the basket and began to spread out the items Cook had sent. Finding the bottle of red wine, she passed it to Trent for him to open and waited with two glasses and watched him pour the wine.

They both took a swallow of wine and watched the water from the bluff. Eugenie passed her husband a plate she had filled with cheese, meats, and bread. They both ate in comfortable silence for a few minutes.

Eugenie decided now was a perfect time to tell him of her suspicions. Here, where he was away from his business and anything else that might distract him. She wanted his complete attention.

"You seem preoccupied," he finally said.

"Do I? I hadn't noticed."

"Liar," he replied with a rude sound coming from deep in his throat. It was sort of cute, but to an outsider, he would sound vulgar.

She nibbled on her cheese as she contemplated how to tell him. "There is something," she finally said.

"I'm listening."

"I believe I'm with child, Trent."

He jerked his head up. "What did you say?"

"I haven't had it confirmed, but I'm certain I'm with child."

He set his wine glass down on the blanket. "Are you sure?"

"I need to see a physician, but yes, I'm sure."

He grinned. "Then perhaps we need to make a stop in London after all."

"I'll be fine to wait until we return to Gloucestershire."

"Are you excited?" he asked. He leaned over and kissed her. "Because I know I am. This is wonderful news."

"Yes, I am."

"This is the best news. Especially today."

Eugenie squealed as he lowered her down on the blanket. "You best watch the wine glasses, my lord."

He leaned over, taking one glass and finishing its contents. His own glass was already empty. He returned to her side and kissed her deeply, a sense of urgency in his actions. "The hell with the wine glasses."

From beneath him, Eugenie moaned, her fingers running through his curls. Her legs opened to him as his hand glided down her legs, bending them at the knee. Slowly, his fingers found what they were after.

"No underwear. Were you expecting dallying with your husband?" he growled.

"A lady can never be too prepared," she replied, her voice ragged. "I want you, Trent. . .now."

He pushed a finger inside her, and she responded. She was wet and ready for him. Quickly, he unfastened his trousers and impaled her. She lifted her hips to meet him as he began the slow dance of coupling. He wanted to enjoy every single second with her. Only Eugenie could make him forget all the unpleasantness he had to deal with. Everything disappeared when he was with her, and for that, he was eternally grateful.

"Ah, Eugenie, you must know you're my heart and soul. I cannot breathe when you're around, and I intend for it to stay like that. Now come, let's finish eating," he finally said. "We'll take a walk along the edge of the bluff, if you like, afterwards."

"I'd like that, and I'm still hungry."

He looked in the basket and found an apple. He began to cut it into wedges, and he watched Eugenie pull off another piece of bread and then reach for more cheese and smoked meats.

"Would you care for another glass of wine?"

"Please."

He poured two fresh glasses of wine and handed her one. As they ate, the wind gusts began to pick up. Eugenie reached for her hat before it blew away. She accepted the wine with her other hand and took a sip.

Trent also sipped his wine before nibbling on a slice of apple. Looking up at the sky he saw it changing. From a cloudless sunny day, the afternoon was becoming clouded, the sun peaking from behind occasionally.

"You made mention there are discrepancies in the books? Do you mean the books for this estate?" she asked.

"Yes."

"Do you think your estate manager is at fault?"

"Yes. He's the only one who keeps the books. I thought I found something last time I was here, and ever since, I've paid close attention to everything the man sends me."

"Hmmm, do you suspect him of profiting from the estate?" she asked. "You know he tried to have a cheaper stove put in. He thought I'd never venture to the kitchens and would never notice the difference."

"I believe that's exactly what's happening here."

"So what are you going to do?"

"Finish my audit, make notes, then call him in to go over the books with me. That's when I'll confront him with my findings."

"And now I understand why you've been spending so many hours in your study and why you've been so ill tempered."

"Yes, and I apologize."

She smiled at him. "No need, though in the future, please tell me what's distressing you. Don't keep it from me. You make my head wander to places it shouldn't."

He put his hand over his heart. "I promise."

He rose from his spot on the blanket and extended his hand to Eugenie, who had just finished putting everything back in the basket. "I hate to break this off, but I think it best we head back."

"Yes, the weather can change quickly."

Taking the basket, Trent led her back to the gig. He helped her into the cart, and they began their journey back to the house. "Next time we'll leave earlier and continue down the main road."

"I understand it goes completely around the island?"

"It does."

She tied her hat tighter as the breeze increased in strength. Trent urged the gelding into a trot in an effort to get them both home safely before the showers began. The last time he dared look to the north, he could see where rain had begun miles away. It wouldn't be long before it reached them.

CHAPTER 18

"*I* know you were wanting to get back to Gloucestershire, but I foresee us staying another fortnight," Trent announced at dinner that evening. He gazed across the table to where Eugenie was seated. He watched her push the roasted chicken around on her plate, taking a small bite now and then.

"Whatever you need to do is fine with me," she replied. "It'll give me time to finish some sketching I've been doing of the gardens."

"You're sure?"

"Yes, I know this has weighed heavily on you, and it needs to be finished and dealt with. I really do like it here, Trent, so no worries."

He hesitated, watching her nibble on a piece of chicken. "I know you'd like to consult with a physician, and I thought we could stay in London a couple of days when we leave."

"Thank you, Trent."

He smiled and reached a hand across to her. "No need. We're in this together. I want you to have the best possible care."

"I suppose you are already sure of what the child is."

"Whatever the babe is will be fine with me. I only wish for a healthy child."

She put her fork down on the plate. "As do I. The child is already letting me know they're there."

"Yes, don't think I haven't noticed you pushing your food around on the plate. I know it's difficult, but you need to eat, Eugenie."

"I'm trying. Nothing much appeals to me."

After dinner, Trent accompanied her to the drawing room. He poured himself a glass of port while waiting on tea to be served. He was about to ask her if she would play something on the piano, but when he glanced over at her, she was sound asleep. He smiled and took a lightweight blanket from the back of one of the settees and covered her with it. He sat in a chair across from her, port in one hand.

When the butler brought the tea service, he put a finger to his lips to let him know to be quiet. He placed the tray on a nearby table and left as quietly as he'd entered. Eugenie never stirred. The day had been full, and he supposed being outside added to her need to sleep, though she'd insist it was being with child making her so.

He took a swallow of the amber liquid and pondered how things were going to play out. He was about finished with his assessment. A solicitor from the firm his family had used for generations was due late tomorrow. The two of them would go over everything Trent had found so far and then discuss how the matter should be taken care of. He didn't like to put anyone out of work, but he disliked there being a thief in his midst even more.

His solicitor had the names of a couple of men he knew to be looking for positions. This position was a lot of times multi-generational, but under the circumstances, Trent felt what the estate needed was new eyes on the books.

Eugenie stirred and opened her eyes. "How long have I been asleep?"

"Not long," he replied. "Would you like for me to pour you some tea?"

She shook her head. "It's been a long day, and I can't seem to keep my eyes open. Would you mind terribly if I retired early?"

"No, not at all," he replied.

"What will you do? Go back to your study to work?"

"Yes," he replied as he offered his hand to help her stand. "I need to have everything in order for when the solicitor arrives."

Nodding, she leaned up and kissed him. "Just don't spend the entire night working. I don't like waking up to an empty bed."

"I promise. I'm about finished anyway."

"Good," she replied, her hand reaching up to pat his cheek. "I expect you to wake me."

He arched a brow. "Does the marchioness have something in mind?"

"Of course. I'm only with child, silly. I still crave my husband."

"Then I guess I'll be forced to oblige." He kissed her. "Sweet dreams, my love."

Eugenie left Trent in the drawing room and lazily made her way upstairs to their bedchamber. Her lady's maid was surprised to see her so early, but much to her credit, had already laid out her mistress's night gown and robe.

She stood quietly as her dress was unbuttoned and removed and her undergarments loosened and removed as well. All she wanted to do was crawl between the sheets and close her eyes. She knew this tiredness was a part of early pregnancy and prayed it would go away as quickly as it had come.

Closing her eyes, she fell asleep as quickly as her head hit the pillow.

Trent, in the meantime, was back in his study. Returning to his desk, he could tell instantly someone had been rifling through what little sat out. He'd put all the estate ledgers and the papers he'd written into the safe before he and Eugenie had left on their picnic earlier. He'd made it abundantly clear with the housekeeper that no one was to clean his study until he finished with a particular project.

Someone wasn't listening, and he didn't like the idea of someone invading his private space. Since Eugenie's run-in with his estate manager, Trent suspected him. The man had been left to answer to no one for far too long. He had to know Trent was onto him. The man hadn't been that clever.

He poured himself a brandy and sat down at the desk and contemplated what he had found so far. Trent felt fortunate he wasn't like some peers who never checked on the affairs of their estates. It was part of the reason a lot of them were running in the red. That and their own careless spending.

He sat back in his chair and put his boots up on the desk. Sipping his brandy, he wondered if he should start working at this late hour or wait until morning. He needed to write letters, but that, too, could wait until tomorrow.

Life had certainly changed for Trent. He was now looking at being a father, something he'd rarely thought about before he'd married Eugenie. He was most fortunate to have a wife whose interests went far beyond the gossip of London drawing rooms.

Once he had this situation taken care of, they would leave for London, and afterwards, back to his country estate. There was certainly enough to keep him busy, and London wasn't that far should he need to meet an associate. He was certain both his father and father-in-law expected him to be more involved. He was. He'd taken care of problems that had arisen from the building of their ship in Southampton. He would write each of them and let them know his schedule and plans. Hopefully, they would take on some of the responsibilities of their ventures once they found out they were going to be grandfathers.

MR. FINCH, a solicitor he'd been working with in regards to this estate, arrived mid-morning having spent the night before at a small hotel in the village. Trent recalled having met the man a few times when he'd been to their London office. He was perhaps ten years older than Trent with thinning, gray hair, a hawkish nose, and wire-framed glasses.

As Eugenie still had not come downstairs, Trent took him directly to his study where they laid out all the ledgers and notes Trent had made. He called for tea while Mr. Finch began scanning the ledgers, looking for anything out of sorts.

Mr. Finch asked few questions at first as he went through Trent's notes and compared them to what was in the ledgers. He shook his head a few times, scribbling furiously on a paper.

"He really did little to hide what he was doing. I would have expected him to keep a second set of books. That's what the good ones do when they're stealing from their employer."

Trent nodded. "He probably thought if I did visit, it would be for short periods of time, and I wouldn't take the time to go through months and months of ledger entries."

"True. What do you intend to do, my lord?"

"What do you suggest?" Trent countered. "My first reaction is to let him go. It's stealing, and I can't allow that from any employee. He's also left a bad impression with me by the way he's treated my wife." Trent went on to explain the incident with the stove, how the man had changed out what Eugenie had wanted.

"Your first reaction would be my suggestion. Fire him. I can give you the names of a couple of men who have been estate managers or would thrive at the chance."

"Why would someone leave their position? It's usually unheard of."

"True, but in this man's case, the owner abandoned the estate after a fire gutted the house. It seemed he had a bit of a gambling problem. Everyone was let go after the fire, and since then he's been working with my firm."

"Ah, but he might well prefer to stay there. What about the other man?"

"He's a peer. Third son of a viscount. When his father's estate manager died, his father let him take over the running of their main estate. He was doing quite well until his father died and his brother became Viscount."

"I can imagine what happened next," Trent remarked.

"His brother decided to hire his own man and let his own brother go. You know how hard it can be for younger sons to find their place. He's quite good with land management and the finances of an estate."

"It sounds like he's the one."

Finch nodded. "He's young, ambitious, and quite knowledgeable in new techniques."

"Let's take care of this situation, then you can write him and set up a meeting. Here, of course."

"If I might be so bold as to suggest something, my lord?"

"Absolutely."

"Speak with both men. Make sure you've chosen the right man for the job."

"Then that's what I'll do," Trent replied. "You'll be here when I speak with each man, won't you?"

"If that is your wish, my lord."

"I'll leave it to you to make the introduction. We can all three speak about certain items, and I can take them about the estate."

"Then let's take care of this business, and I'll write each gentleman inviting them. A day apart from the other."

"Excellent idea."

Trent invited Finch for luncheon as there were other matters from the other properties that needed discussing. He noted Finch seemed pleased Trent took such an interest in the running of his estates. And Trent did. They gave him purpose because he knew if he left them in good order once he became marquess, his successor wouldn't have to walk into a mess.

The next day Finch was present when Trent called the estate manager in and let him go. He was surprised at the man's lack of reaction at being caught. He didn't make excuses or try and defend himself. He knew his misdeeds had finally caught up with him. Trent let him go without references. It was the best he could do without involving the local police, and he knew the man was grateful for that.

WITH A LOT ON HIS MIND, his head swimming with figures, Trent was paying no attention to what was going on around him when he entered White's on a rainy afternoon. He was to meet his friends, Radstock and Preston for drinks, conversation, and a late lunch.

He descended his carriage, only to have his path blocked by none other than the Duke of Northshire. The man had a lot of nerve even approaching him. Trent stared him in the eye, careful to make sure his face showed no emotion whatsoever.

"Trent," the duke said with a smirk. "I believe you have something of mine?"

"Really?" Trent countered, the rain running off his hat. "I can't think of what it might be. Now, if you'll excuse me, I'd like to get out of the rain."

The duke blocked him, forcing him to continue standing on the sidewalk, which in spite of the rain, was fairly busy. "Not so fast."

"Northshire, you abducted my wife. I should have had you brought up on charges."

Neither man moved.

"She wasn't your wife, and I didn't abduct her," the duke drawled.

"Really? What would you call it?"

You held her against her will, threatened her. . .should I go on?"

"Of course she would tell you that. I can assure you there was no abduction. Eugenie came with me willingly. We were on our way to be married by my brother, the vicar."

"Lady Trent to you, Northshire. How can you be so naive? You abducted her from the theater, took her to some remote hunting lodge, and kept her locked in a windowless room. If that's how you treat your betrothed, I would hate to see how you'd treat your wife."

"I would expect her to say as much. All untrue."

Trent felt his fist ball up tight at his side as he tried to keep his temper in check. "I have nothing to say to you, Your Grace. Now if you'll excuse me."

"I'm afraid I'm not finished, Trent. Lady Eugenie and I were to be married."

Trent laughed, interrupting Northshire and making the duke's face darken. "Except you never asked for her. You never met with her father."

"That's because we were eloping. I had a special license arranged, and as I mentioned, my brother was to wed us."

"I don't have time for this nonsense," Trent replied wearily. All he wanted was to get in out of the rain, and away from this mad man. He tried to step around the duke but was once again blocked. This time by one of the duke's men.

"This is what you're going to do, Lord Trent. You're going to ask for an annulment. On what grounds matters not to me. You will sign over her dowry to me, and I shall marry her."

The duke was either broke or in great need of funds. Trent had heard rumors the duke liked games of chance and cards. Evidently, too much. The man wasn't going to stand here and threaten him or his wife.

Trent closed the distance between them, getting in the duke's face. "No, I'll not. Find yourself some other young chit, if anyone will have you. You'll stay away from my wife or I'll have you brought up on charges of kidnapping. Do I make myself clear, Your Grace?"

Northshire smirked. "I compromised your wife, Trent. When we were staying in the cottage. Only she wasn't your wife then."

Trent's fist met the duke's face with force. Northshire stumbled backwards, and his hand flew up to his jaw in disbelief.

"Stay away from my wife," Trent spat. "If I hear you've spoken about her in anything but a glowing manner, I will make good on my threat."

As he began to walk away a path parted for Trent.

His hand throbbed, but for the first time, he felt satisfaction. Northshire had been allowed to get away with it because no one wished to bring a duke up on charges. He imagined Northshire would scurry out of town to one of his estates to hide.

Good riddance.

THREE WEEKS later Trent and Eugenie were back at Gloucestershire. Their stop in London had been brief, giving Eugenie time to consult with a physician about her condition and Trent time to do the things gentlemen did.

He spent time at his solicitors, meeting about the ship. He went to Tattersalls one afternoon where he found nothing to his satisfaction if one compared them to his own bloodlines. Trent also visited Whites to meet friends, eat, and enjoy some conversation and catch up on what was going on.

Most of all, he was happy to return to Trent Manor. The tree-lined drive welcomed them as the carriage rolled toward the house. The carriage stopped, and Trent jumped out, looking up at the house. He turned to assist Eugenie out of the carriage.

She looked up at the grand manor and smiled. "It's good to be home, isn't it?"

"It certainly is," he replied, his arm around her waist as he escorted her to the stairs leading to the front door.

EPILOGUE

GLOUCESTERSHIRE, 6 MONTHS LATER

*L*ady Victoria Eugenie Anne Trent made her entrance into the world in the middle of a late January snowstorm. She let all around her know of her arrival the moment she took her first breath.

She was followed approximately three minutes later by her more subdued brother, Lord Percival Andrew Mortimer Charles Trent.

Trent had sat outside his wife's bedchamber waiting for news, as the midwife was not progressive when it came to birthing children. Men got in the way and had no place while their wives were giving birth.

The moment he heard his daughter's loud cry, he was on his feet. His old friend Viscount Radstock, who'd been visiting with his bride, the Lady Lucinda, clapped his friend on the back.

"Well done!" Radstock crowed.

Then a second, quieter cry. Both men looked at the other.

"Twins?" Trent mused.

At that very moment, Lady Lucinda appeared, closing the door behind her. She was smiling widely.

"You have a daughter and a son, my lord. Congratulations."

Trent sat down, afraid his legs wouldn't hold him. "Twins?"

"Yes, and they're very healthy, as you can hear. You can see them momentarily, as soon as they've been cleaned up."

"How is Eugenie? Is she all right?"

"She is fine. Tired, but made it through the birth without incident," Lucinda replied. She was an exquisite creature, and if he weren't happily married, and if Radstock hadn't already married her, he might have pursued her. She had flax colored hair with the most amazing violet eyes. "You can see her in a moment as well."

Radstock handed Trent a glass of whiskey as they watched Radstock's wife disappear back into the bedchamber.

"Here's to being a father. You're going to be the best," Radstock said.

Trent drank the whiskey in one swallow. "Twins."

"You have one of each, and fortunately, one is a boy, so you've got your heir."

Trent walked over to the small table where the crystal decanter sat and poured himself another. Just as he was about to take a sip, one of the attending ladies came out of the bedchamber.

"Lord Trent, would you like to meet your babies?"

Trent nodded; words would not come. The room wasn't dark as Trent expected. No, Eugenie had insisted the draperies be open and the daylight let in. He walked over to the bed and leaned down and kissed his wife.

"You're okay?"

"I'm fine," she replied. "Go meet your son and daughter."

He walked over to the cradle which the two babes were sharing at the moment. Both appeared sound asleep, that is until his daughter opened her eyes and began wailing. A nurse went to quiet her, and Trent instinctively reached out for her.

The moment she was in his arms, she quieted.

"Oh my," Eugenie said. "Someone's already got their father wrapped around their little finger."

"She's beautiful," was all Trent could say. He walked to the window and back before handing one babe off for the other.

His son favored his mother even at this tender young age. Though his eyes were closed, and he had little hair, his facial features mirrored Eugenie. His daughter, on the other hand, appeared to favor him more, though he saw some of Eugenie in her as well.

"They're both beautiful," he said. "What are we going to name them?"

"Since we picked out one for a boy and one for a girl, we'll go with them. We can call him Andrew or Charles. I know how much you dislike Percival."

"I do, and I believe him to look like Andrew."

"Very well, Andrew it is," she replied.

The midwife cleared her throat, causing Trent to swing his head in her direction. "My lord, your wife needs to rest. She's been through quite an ordeal."

He glanced at Eugenie, who was trying desperately not to laugh. "Yes, of course." He turned his attention to his wife. "Sleep, my love. I'll visit you later."

"I'll see you then. Now, go entertain our guests, who I imagine never thought they'd be part of all this."

"No, I'm sure they didn't, just being married and all."

"Maybe it'll get Radstock busy."

Trent smiled as he opened the door. "Somehow, I think he's been very busy since his wedding."

Radstock met him in the large hallway. "How is Eugenie? And the babes?"

"She's fine, and they are beautiful," he replied.

"Come, let's celebrate. Cigars and brandy await, and Lucinda has gone to see a feast is prepared for tonight's meal."

"I'm grateful for you being here. I was rather dreading sending for my father. I'm sure I would have had to sit through his stories of when my sister and I were born."

"Somehow I believe every man does just that," he replied. "You should send word to your parents. Eugenie's as well."

"I will this evening. I would just like some quiet time with my new family. Not that you and Lucinda are a bother in any sense of the word. You know our parents. They'll all descend on us as soon as clothes can be packed, and I'm not quite ready for all that."

As he and his old friend sat in his study, smoking cigars and enjoying French brandy, Trent couldn't get over how much his life had changed in such a short period of time. He was happier and more content than he'd ever been.

And Lady Eugenie? As though motherhood wasn't enough, Trent had found the perfect location, in the village for his wife to finally fulfill her long-time dream of seeing less fortunate children were education. He'd yet to tell her, that was a gift to her. Once she recovered from childbirth he would surprise her.

The next generation had arrived.

ALSO BY JR SALISBURY

MAYFAIR

Dealing with the Duchess

Ravaging the Duke

To Love An Earl

The Marquess Takes A Bride

MACLEODS OF SKYE

Donnan's Rose

The Sins of Rory MacLeod

Lord Malcolm's Heart

Taming Lily

The Wicked Seduction of Wallace MacLeod

LOVE AND DEVOTION

Wish Upon A Duke

Once Upon A Countess

Seduction of a Duke

Second Chance At Love

ABOUT THE AUTHOR

J. R. Salisbury is the historical romance alter-ego of contemporary romance author Jamie Salisbury. Writing romance stories with passion and sass, Jamie Salisbury has seen several of her books soar to #1 on Amazon. Her novella, Tudor Rubato was a finalist in the 2012 RONE awards. The cover won for Best Contemporary Cover. In 2014, her novel, Life and Lies was nominated for a RONE in the Erotica category. Her books are self published.

Music, traveling and history are among her passions when not writing. Her previous career in public relations in and around the entertainment field has afforded her with a treasure trove of endless story ideas.

Follow Jamie:
Book + Main
Website

Facebook as Jamie Salisbury

www.ingramcontent.com/pod-product-compliance
Lightning Source LLC
Chambersburg PA
CBHW011517100726
47899CB00010BD/3400